I0623833

DARK FURY

Return of the Huntress

Gemma Jaeger: Huntress of the Preternatural
Book 1

MONIQUE J SIEDLAK

OSHUN
PUBLICATIONS
oshunpublications.com

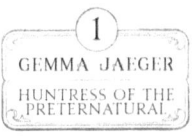

1

GEMMA JAEGER

HUNTRESS OF THE
PRETERNATURAL

RETURN OF THE HUNTRESS

DARK FURY

MONIQUE J SIEDLAK

Dark Fury: Return of the Huntress by Monique J. Siedlak

Published by Oshun Publications
9 Old Kings Road STE. 123 #1038
Palm Coast, FL 32137
www.oshunpublications.com

ISBN 978-1-950378-65-4 (Paperback)
ISBN 978-1-956319-35-4 (Hardback)
ISBN 978-1-950378-64-7 (eBook)

Book design by Deranged Doctor Design
www.derangeddoctordesign.com

JOIN MY
NEWSLETTER
GET UPDATES,
FREEBIES &
GIVEAWAYS
MOJOSIEDLAK.COM/NOCTURNECHRONICLES

Audiobook
Coming in 2024

mojosiedlak.com/Dark_Fury_Book

CHAPTER 1

GEMMA JAEGER CLUTCHED A BOTTLE OF ABSINTHE BY THE neck, tight enough to shatter the glass. She stared at it in her hand. What she would give to just down it and let the liquid spread throughout her body, numbing the pain that still felt fresh.

It was the fifth anniversary of her parents' death.

But, no, she wouldn't be wallowing in her sorrows tonight, and drowning her guilt and emptiness with alcohol was no longer how she coped.

She glanced around the Moonlight Bar. This was *her* bar. Usually a source of great pride. But now she groaned.

Why had she ever agreed to host the bachelorette party for Drew, one of her bartenders, tonight of all nights?

As if Gemma's thoughts had summoned her, the bride-to-be approached. Nodding at the Absinthe with bright eyes, she waggled her brows. "That for us?"

"Uh, no," Gemma said, returning the premium bottle to its place on the top shelf behind her. "But how about another round of wine coolers?"

"Yes, please." Drew grinned.

"Are you having a good time?" she asked Drew in the

most cheerful voice she could muster, while fighting off the competing waves of nausea and grief.

"This party is amazing," Drew gushed. Her forehead glistened with a sheen of sweat and her cheeks were flushed from spending the last few hours on the makeshift dance floor. "Thank you again so much for letting us have it here."

"It was no problem at all," Gemma quickly responded —a lie. Her resentment still lingered beneath the surface of the pleasant smile she flashed at Drew.

A five-alarm fire destroyed the original venue for Drew's party two nights earlier. With no alternative locations to hold it available at the last minute, Gemma offered up the bar. But she hadn't planned for the partygoers to be hellbent on roping her into the festivities. She'd expected to sit on a bar stool at the periphery. Keep an eye on things. Make sure no one got too rowdy or fall-down drunk or trashed the place. But as it stood, Drew was treating her like a bridesmaid instead of a boss. She'd dragged Gemma around to meet all of her friends, begged her to do shots with them, and even tried to convince her to participate in a karaoke duet. It took everything inside Gemma to keep up a semi-happy façade and not destroy the mood with her glum self-pity.

But she didn't know how much more socializing she could handle.

"And there she is. Miss Gemma Jaeger!"

Gemma heard the familiar voice from the other side of the bar and froze.

I have got to be hearing things, she thought.

This couldn't be happening.

She couldn't face him.

Especially today of all days.

Her heart thudded in her chest. She turned slowly away from Drew and toward the front door.

"Randy?" Gemma whispered.

Her eyes landed on the man who'd called out. She stared at him as if he were a mirage that would disappear if she focused hard enough. But he didn't. She blinked.

It wasn't a coincidence that Randy Silverman had shown up tonight. She pushed down the shock of seeing him, and the sting of memories that came along with his presence. She pulled on the masked expression that hid her true emotions and willed it not to slip out of place. "Oh my god! It's been such a long time!"

She found herself unable to move, but that was okay. In several long, certain strides, he closed the distance between them.

"Too long," he said, his voice gruff.

Randy Silverman had the rugged face of a Hunter. He wasn't in the best of shape anymore. Could benefit from losing a few pounds. But she had no doubt that he was still a force to be reckoned with, mentally and physically. Rough around the edges with brawny arms and calloused fingers, sharp-eyed Randy was the kind of man who preferred his hands dirty. The kind of man who would kill for the people he loved.

"I've missed you, girl." Randy wrapped her in one of his signature bear hugs.

He smelled of cigar smoke and woodsy cologne; a nostalgic and wistful scent that both overwhelmed and comforted Gemma when she breathed it in.

Gemma didn't know what to say. The heat of shame crept up the back of her neck until it set her cheeks aflame. It *had* been a long time, way too long, and there was no one to blame for that but herself. Randy had been a dear friend of her parents. He'd always been like an honorary uncle to her. Randy had tried to reach out to her many times since that tragic day, but she'd shot down every attempt. It wasn't personal. She didn't speak to much of anyone from the past anymore. It was her, not them.

"I heard about you opening this place a while back. I didn't know if you just needed space or if my invite got lost in the mail."

As he spoke, his gaze swept the room from corner to corner. It was a Hunter's instinct, she knew, to always be hyper aware of your surroundings.

"You never returned any of my calls, so I assumed it was the former and stayed away," he said.

Until now, Gemma thought.

She was still grappling with the reality that he was really standing in front of her, in her bar. Tonight, of all nights, when she was most vulnerable and least equipped to deal with a blast from the past.

"You could have just dropped in any time," she told him, though they both knew the sentiment was half-hearted at best. "Sort of like…"

He ducked his head, clearly not proud of how he'd burst back into her life without warning. "Tonight? Yeah. I know you probably would have preferred to be alone today, but I worry about you. Always have."

Gemma's heart deflated in her chest. "I know, Randy."

She was sorry to keep everyone at arm's length, but it just was easier for her.

"I heard you're out of the life?" Randy asked.

Scanning the room for eavesdroppers, Gemma saw that the partiers barely even seemed to register that she'd stepped away. Her tense shoulders relaxed a bit. "Yeah, I am. And I don't talk about it, actually. You're the first Hunter I've even seen in ages, so…"

He smiled a sad smile that told her he'd have left the

life long ago, too, if he thought he could. "Yeah. I've heard rumors our kind aren't all that welcome here."

"It's not that… It's just…" Gemma shook her head.

It was just that. It was exactly that.

Randy squeezed her elbow. "Just teasing you, kid. I get it. I do. But this particular Hunter ain't leaving until you tell him how you *really* are."

Gemma did not want to have this conversation, but something about Randy lowered her defenses. She hadn't wanted him to come. But now that he was here, she didn't really want him to leave. After grabbing him a beer, Gemma led Randy to a table away from everyone else to sit and talk.

"Some days are harder than others. This is one of those harder days," she admitted as they settled in.

"Your parents…" He took a long drink before continuing. "They were good people. They would be proud of you."

She wasn't sure about that. There wasn't a whole lot to be proud of. Gemma had turned her back on her family's legacy. She hadn't even spoken a word to her younger sister since Danielle left East Haven. Feeling abandoned and adrift, liquor had been her only friend for a while. That is, at least, until Matt Silva came back into the picture.

As if on cue, the bells over the door chimed. Gemma looked up as Matt stopped just inside to shrug off his jacket and hang it on the coat rack. Their eyes met. His smile lit up his entire face. He started towards her and Randy.

Gemma sprang from her chair.

"I'll be right back," she told Randy.

She strode quickly towards Matt, cutting him off before he reached their table.

"Did I come at a bad time?" Matt asked. His eyebrows rose as he seemed to study Randy over her shoulder.

Gemma didn't want to lie to Matt, but there were things—the things she and Randy had been talking about —he couldn't ever know about. There were parts of her that needed to remain in the past. Buried. Just like her parents.

"Not at all," she said, with a forced and faltering smile. She hoped the tightness she felt in her entire body wasn't reflected on her face. "Come meet an old friend of the family."

"Your family?" Matt's voice was filled with surprise.

"Yes." Her voice was tight now, too, as she turned and made her way back to Randy. She could only hope he would follow her conversational lead and drop the topics they'd previously been catching up on.

"Randy," she said. "This is my friend, Matt Silva. Matt, this is Randy Silverman, an old friend of my family."

Randy briefly lifted his chin in a greeting. "We go way back, me and Gemma."

"So do Gemma and I," Matt replied, lightly.

"Huh. I don't remember ever hearing your name before," Randy remarked. His hands were locked together on the table, and his eyes pinned Matt in place, staring him down. It was as if Randy saw Matt as the outsider here, and he expected him to prove that he wasn't a threat. Like a wolf protecting their pup. Or like he was challenging Matt to a duel for territorial rights.

Matt's eyes shifted to her, pleading.

"Randy, stop." She nudged him not so gently. "You're making Matt uncomfortable."

Gemma gestured for Matt to sit. She pulled up a third chair from an empty nearby table for herself.

"I guess he hasn't heard too much about me either, huh?" Randy asked.

Gemma shook her head. Randy nodded, shooting her a look of understanding.

Matt cleared his throat. "It's nice to meet you, though."

"So, Gemma," Randy began, while keeping his focus on Matt. "You said this fella's your *friend*, now? How good of a friend is he, exactly? Like the kind of friend your dad would want me to take out back and rough up or—"

Despite everything, Gemma almost snorted. She'd never needed a man to rough up anyone *for* her.

"We're just…" Matt interrupted. "Friends." He looked at Gemma for confirmation. She gave an almost imperceptible nod. *Ding, ding, ding. Right answer.* "That's all."

"Huh." Randy took a long pull of his beer.

Out of the corner of her eye, Gemma could see that Matt wasn't squirming yet—but he was close.

"Randy." Gemma laughed, despite herself. "Drop the intimidation act. Matt and I went to school together," she added. "He not only remodeled this place, but he also did work upstairs, converting the empty space into my apartment."

"You don't say. You a contractor?" Randy asked Matt.

"You a detective?" Matt shot back and Randy chuckled. He pointed his bottle at Matt.

"Touché." Randy looked around; his lips pressed tight as he nodded. Matt's work on the bar, at least, seemed to impress him. Even if he wasn't quite as wowed by Matt himself.

"Matt's a reporter," Gemma said. "He does the other stuff on the side. But he's incredibly talented at everything he does."

She hadn't meant to word it quite like that. *Was Matt blushing?*

An awkward silence fell over the group. Matt shifted in his seat. "Speaking of work, I should, uh, make a few phone calls. Important project coming up." He stood quite quickly, nearly knocking over his chair in the meantime. "You two catch up. I'll be back in a few."

As soon as he was gone, Randy leaned forward on his elbows. His serious expression cracked into a grin. "Was he going to make calls or change into dry pants?"

She shook her head, shooting Randy a look of admonishment. Then she watched with fondness as Matt walked toward the stairs that led up to her apartment. "He's a good guy, Randy."

Matt was more than good to her, and he'd really helped her out a lot since they'd reconnected.

No, it was more than that. Most likely, she literally wouldn't be alive today without him.

"If he's such a good guy, why's he just a friend?" Randy raised an eyebrow.

Gemma blew out a breath and followed it with a noncommittal shrug.

"He doesn't know," Randy surmised.

"No," she said as if it was another exhale. "No one does. You were right. After I first opened up, a few Hunters came around. I may've made them feel like I didn't want them here. And since then, they've stayed away."

The Hunters were a tight-knit community and word traveled fast amongst them.

Laughing, Randy replied while pointing to himself, "Until this bad penny decided to show up." She could tell from the way he eyed her that she was an enigma to him now. "You don't miss it? At all?"

When Gemma thought about hunting again, she couldn't imagine it. She'd been raised to hunt, but other than one necessary case, she'd never hunted without her parents and Danielle. She didn't know how to walk that path alone. Or if she even wanted to.

But *did* she miss it?

That was a cactus of a question. Impossible to try to handle without a whole lot of sting.

She waved her hand around them. "I've put all my blood, sweat, and tears into this place. It's my livelihood. It's my home. And it's all I have time or energy for at the moment."

Randy took a big breath and leaned back in his chair. "Too bad. You get a bunch of Hunters around a campfire, someone's going to tell a tale about the amazing Jaegers. Your family will go down in history as one of the best."

"Key word there is history, Rand. My family *was* one of the best," she corrected him. "That's all done with now."

She sat up and squared her shoulders, attempting to look more certain than she felt.

I have no family. It's just me.

Randy reached out and held one of her trembling hands in his. "Speaking of family, how's your sister?"

Gemma swallowed the bitterness that rose in her throat. She didn't want to go there. She couldn't tonight. The memory of her parents was enough.

"You'd have to ask her," she said, finally. "I wouldn't know."

It had been five years since her parents were murdered. And almost that long since she'd seen her sister.

After a long moment of silence, Randy chugged down the remainder of his beer. "It looks like you've got quite a few inebriated gals about to start a conga line. So I'm gonna get out of your hair and let you deal with that." He stood. "How much for the beer?"

"The beer is on the house," she said, getting to her feet, too. "And the one next time will be, as well.

"You mean that?" he asked with an almost sheepish

smile. "Because it's been great seeing you, Gemma."

Returning his smile, she opened her arms to him, wanting—maybe even needing—another one of his embraces. "Believe it or not, I feel the same."

"If you ever need me for anything, anything at all," he said before he pulled away. "Please, call me. My number hasn't changed."

"That's good to know," she said.

"So, use it, mmkay?"

She nodded, with a lump in her throat.

Randy pulled Gemma back into a hug, holding her tight, like she was the daughter he never had and always wanted. In that moment, Gemma's heart lurched. Wrapped in his strong arms, she became aware of how long it had been since she had been around someone who knew her the way Randy did. She saw in his eyes how much he cared for her, and it brought up feelings she had been keeping at bay. Feelings from a time when people loved her.

"I know you've got Mr. Just A Friend, but if you ever need someone to talk to, someone who knows it all, I'm here for you."

"I may've forgotten for a minute, Randy, but I'm glad you stopped in to remind me."

Gemma swallowed hard. Unless you counted Danielle —and she didn't—Randy was the closest thing she had left to family. And she had pushed him away.

And I shouldn't have, she thought.

But the temporary moment of sentimental weakness quickly waned. As she watched Randy walk away and she came back to her senses. She couldn't let herself get reconnected with that life, not even if it meant she had to let go of people who truly knew her and truly loved her, people like Randy.

Gemma stood stock-still for a few minutes, even as the disorganized conga line snaked around her. She couldn't take her eyes off the door where Randy had exited. Tears welled in her eyes and threatened to spill over. She reached up and swatted them away. There had been too much crying for a life long gone. There would be no more.

"Did Randy leave already?"

Gemma turned to see Matt approaching, with two bottles of flavored sparkling water. He handed her one.

"Yeah," she said, opening it and taking a sip. The hint of lime was refreshing on her tongue. It would kill her thirst, but not her memories. She glanced back at the bottle of Absinthe, before committing her attention to Matt.

"I have two questions. First, did you enjoy your visit?"

"I think it was something I needed," she replied, giving him a forced smile. "What's the second question?"

"Is he always so scary? I half-expected him to pull out a shotgun and demand to know what my intentions are towards you."

This time, her grin was real. "That performance was solely for you. He's a teddy bear."

"Are you sure you don't mean a grizzly bear?" Matt asked.

Gemma laughed. "Come on. It's closing time."

Gemma didn't enjoy being a buzz kill, but she'd made it clear to Drew in advance what hour party time would come to an end. In a nice but firm voice, she informed everyone it was time to gather their things and go. She received several good-natured boos and a sloppy, tearful *thank you* hug from Drew. Then the bridal party stumbled out into the night. Thankfully, they had rented several stretch limos to see them home safely, so she didn't have to worry about anyone driving under the influence.

"How are you feeling?" Matt asked, after the place emptied out.

He and Gemma each took a bar cloth and wiped down their respective sides of the bar.

"Well, seeing Randy was good," she said. Matt threw her a skeptical look, prompting her to bat at his arm. "It really was, so stop worrying."

"When did you last see him?"

"At the funeral." She tried to sound matter of fact about it, but her voice wavered a little.

"But he lives pretty close, right?"

"Yep."

"Do you want to talk about it?" Matt's voice was a gentle invitation.

"Nope."

She could tell he was hoping she would let down the walls she'd erected between herself and the rest of the world. Would he ever learn to quit trying? She didn't know. But she needed her walls. They were what kept her safe. That was a fact.

"Right now," she said. "I just want to put this day behind me and start tomorrow fresh."

"I think I can help you with that," he said closing the distance between them and sliding an arm around her waist. "If you don't mind having company tonight."

She shrugged out of his attempted embrace with a sigh.

"Company tonight… isn't something I want."

"But—"

For Gemma Jaeger, being alone with her thoughts like this was dangerous and she knew it.

"But," she echoed, interrupting Matt's protest, "company might be something I need."

CHAPTER 2

"How about I make us a pot of coffee and you can tell me about your day?" Matt suggested as soon as they were upstairs in her apartment.

But she didn't want to rehash her day. She wanted to *forget* it.

And Matt wouldn't want to talk about *his* day, because he was increasingly dissatisfied with his job at the local paper.

"How about you get naked and join me in bed?" Gemma countered, as she pulled her shirt over her head. She wasn't wearing a bra.

Already halfway to her tiny kitchen, Matt glanced over his shoulder. She unbuttoned her jeans and shucked them off.

She stood for a moment, watching as his eyes traveled down her body. His gaze stalled on her breasts before drifting on. She'd only left her panties for him to remove and hoped he'd give into the temptation to rid her of them quickly and quietly.

Cocking an eyebrow at him, she shrugged as if it didn't matter either way.

She meandered to her bed.

Matt followed.

As soon as she'd lain down, he pounced. He crawled onto the mattress, his fully clothed body hovering over her nearly nude form. His pupils dilated, a lustful fog clouding the deep amber of his eyes. He dipped his head and she shuddered with bliss as he swirled his tongue around the tight bud of her right nipple. His hand closed over her left breast, eliciting a moan of pleasure. Longing flooded her body at his touch, the way it always did. The tingle between her thighs would soon be an undeniable demand.

Damn, this man turned her on.

"So…" he said, raising himself back up and gazing down at her. "I'm going to assume you don't want to talk?"

"I think," she paused. "I think there are better things you could be doing with your mouth right now."

"If that's what you need, I am happy to oblige," he said. His hands slid down her body, hooking the sides of her panties with his nimble fingers and lowering them to her ankles. Her knees all but fell open for him, exposing her glistening desire. "So beautiful," he whispered, with a tinge of reverence to his voice she'd never get used to. Sometimes it made her feel uncomfortable. Sometimes it made her want him so badly it hurt.

Her back arched of its own volition as he touched her, not exactly where she wanted him to but close enough to make her whimper. Her chest was already beginning to heave with each breath she took. She wasn't yet panting but knew he'd take her there.

"I wonder," he said, dipping a finger inside her only to immediately pull away. "If you taste as delicious as you look."

"This is not your first rodeo," she said through clenched teeth. The desperation to completely lose control clawed at her. She needed to lose her thoughts, her worries, herself. "And this is not the time to play around. You know what I taste like. Now, Matt. Please."

"Always in a rush." He laughed as he pulled his shirt over his head.

She wriggled, reaching until she could palm the crotch of his jeans, the denim straining from his erection. He was so hard, so…

She swallowed; her mouth dry, as she pictured his length, his girth.

"Take off your pants, too," she rasped. "After you make me come with your mouth, I'm gonna need you to do it again with… other parts of your body."

"Miss Gemma Jaeger, your wish is my command," he said, removing her fumbling fingers from his zipper so he could deftly pull it down.

HALF AN HOUR LATER, they lay next to each other, spent. It hadn't been their longest session by far, but it had been one of the most enthusiastic. Curled against him with her head on his chest, his arm around her, his hand playing in her hair, Gemma was content. Her body was satiated, her mind quiet.

"You know, Gemma," Matt began, out of nowhere, just when she'd hoped they were both within sleep's reach. "One of these days, you're going to have to let someone in. I hope that person is me."

She let out a slow breath.

"Literally just let you in, Matt," she said, lightly. "In and out. And in and out…"

He chuckled, but he pulled her even closer. He kissed her temple. "I'm being serious."

She sighed at his low, soft tone. "I know. I know you

are. And you know I consider you my best friend. You're the only person I confide in."

"No. I'm the only person that you tell just enough to. You don't tell me everything," Matt paused, and then took a deep breath. "But I wish you would."

She remained silent.

What could she say?

That she could fall in love with him if she let herself?

She wasn't going to let herself, ever, so that would only hurt him more.

She'd often wondered if letting him go from a friend to a friend with benefits had been a mistake. She was aware of his feelings for her, and never wanted to lead him on. But she'd been clear, from the beginning, what parts of her he could have and the ones that were off-limits, like her heart and much of what was in her head.

"Today is just… the worst. You know that," she said.

"Well. Yeah. But it's not all bad. Think about the good."

She pushed herself up and looked down at him, her eyebrows arched, her expression demanding an explanation for that absurd remark.

"I know this is the anniversary of your parents' death. But it's another anniversary now, too, Gems. It's the anniversary of your choosing sobriety. Of your choosing yourself. Of your choosing life," he said. "You should be happy about that."

"Well, I wouldn't necessarily say, I *chose* sobriety."

Last year on the day before the anniversary of her parents' death, Gemma nearly drank herself to death. She'd started drinking the morning before and hadn't stopped until she passed out. She didn't want to face the next sunrise. She didn't want another year to pass since she'd lost her parents. Thinking back on it, she wasn't even sure that, in that moment, she wanted to live.

Matt showed up the next morning, on the actual anniversary, even though she'd told him not to. They'd gotten into the habit of having breakfast together. He'd bring breakfast burritos or doughnuts and she'd have the coffee waiting in the bar. When she wasn't there, he'd come upstairs to find her. If he hadn't, she'd be dead.

She didn't remember anything from that day except waking up in the county hospital with Matt beside her bed. *Alcohol poisoning*, the doctors had said. Matt told her he recognized the signs. That it wasn't his first time dealing with an alcoholic. He told her that she may not be so lucky the next time, and she needed to get her act together while she still could. He didn't pressure her or give her an ultimatum. He didn't make her feel ashamed or guilty. He didn't ask her to do it for him. *You need to do it for yourself, because you want to,* he'd said.

Gemma had completed a difficult but successful stint in rehab. She hadn't had a drop of alcohol since the day it almost killed her. Though it wasn't easy, especially since she owned a bar. It would've been easier to sell the bar. To get a job that paid the bills without daily testing her biggest weakness. Some people—like Matt—would say it was downright masochistic to keep running and living above the Moonlight. She understood the worry, but she felt the undeniable need to fight this particular demon head-on every day and not let it win. She supposed it was the Hunter's blood in her veins. Hiding from the monsters only let them win.

She chose not to look at alcohol as the problem. Avoiding alcohol? Sure, that would keep her from drinking. But what about the next thing she happened upon that eased her pain? What was to keep her from getting

addicted to that, instead? If she saw herself as the problem, or the problem as an issue that existed within herself,
though… Well. She could work with that. She could work
on herself.

"You've come so far, Gems," Matt said, as if reading
her mind.

Have I?

She nuzzled against him. "I don't know if I would have
gotten this far without you."

"Of course, you would've. You're tough. But just
because you could shoulder it all on your own, doesn't
mean you have to," Matt said as he held her close, his
fingers stroking up and down her arm like he was lightly
strumming a guitar. "Remember, it's one day at a time."

"Yes, one day at a time." That had been one of her
takeaways from the program. She'd always be an alcoholic.
The key to not being an active alcoholic was paying attention to each step and not the giant, never-ending mountain
she was climbing. There was no reaching the peak. The
goal was to get further away from rock bottom.

"And I want to be here for you, every one of those
days," Matt whispered.

Gemma wanted that, too, but she'd never say it out
loud. It would be like tempting fate. She did not need to
give this cruel world a reason to take someone else
from her.

"I know sometimes I don't say it enough, but I really
am glad you came back into my life when you did," she
whispered.

Matt kissed her forehead softly.

Within a few moments, his breathing changed.

He was asleep, leaving her alone with her thoughts.
Thankfully, those thoughts were of him.

When Gemma had known him in elementary school,

Matt Silva had been a lanky kid whose head was still a bit too big for his body, with long, gangly arms and legs. His family had moved before middle school, so he and Gemma hadn't seen each other for well over a decade when he'd had shown up on her doorstep as a grown ass man. A grown ass fine-looking man. He'd been there in response to an ad she'd put in the paper, seeking a cheap repairman to help with the restoration of the bar she'd just bought.

Back then, alcohol consumed her life. That first drink of the day had been the reason she got out of bed. She needed that first drink so bad she'd started leaving a glass of whisky by her bed, but inevitably, it never made it until morning. She was belligerent and belittling to anyone who came near her, the pain of her parents' death a poison eating away at her insides and spewing out of her mouth. She couldn't even acknowledge her sister's absence back then, not without inviting in thoughts too dark even for her. It was just a rotting ache in her soul she ignored, the loneliness giving more strength to the vitriol she spat at who dared glance her way.

But Matt refused to be pushed away. He took the job. He took her snark, her angry outbursts, and her demeaning comments in stride. He kept working, kept showing up day after day. Finally, even she couldn't handle how shitty she was being to him anymore, even if it didn't seem to faze him at all.

"What the hell is wrong with you?" she'd asked one evening, when he was wrapping up to head home. She was already good and buzzed—and she was a mean drunk—with no doubt he'd be back the next morning, anyway. "Why are you still here, putting up with my bullshit? I criticize everything you do. I nitpick. I'm bitchy."

He shook his head, placing his tools in his tool bag. "I don't know, Gems. I guess because I know that under all that façade you're putting up, you're still that little girl with the afro puffs who always had to swing higher than me, run faster than me, climb one more tree branch farther than I dared."

She let out an exasperated sigh and crossed her arms, which caused her to stumble a little. He reached out, placing his hands on her shoulders to steady her. She jerked away. "So, I was an ass to you then and I'm a bigger ass to you now. What's your point?"

"You were cute as hell with that competitive nature and those afro puffs back then. Yes, you're kind of an ass right now, but I don't judge people based on their worst days."

Taken aback, she opened her mouth to reply with a nasty comment, but Matt interrupted her.

"Do you remember Terrence?" Matt looked up from where he knelt next to his bag. They made eye contact before he zipped it and slung the strap over his shoulder.

She did remember Terrence.

"I hated that guy. Ugh."

He was your classic playground bully, and after the vile things he'd put her classmates through, she secretly hoped he'd ended up with premature baldness with a beer gut.

"Everyone hated him," Matt said, standing. "But *you*." He wagged his finger at her. "You, Gemma Jaeger, were the only one who ever stood up to him."

She shrugged her shoulders. "So?"

"So, in third grade, I was the new kid, which made me his primary target. I was swinging one day, and he stomped over. Shoved me out of my swing and onto the ground. You were on the jungle gym and saw it go down. You jumped down, stormed over, and gave him a talking-to that would make a grown man cower. The kind of talking-to you give me on the daily now."

Matt shook his head.

"You were wearing a pink dress. Had skinned knees. You had fire in your eyes back then. You have a fierce bark, but I don't see that fire now," he paused. "I'd like to, though."

Gemma looked down at the ground, too tipsy to really comprehend what he was saying but sober enough to understand that his words *meant* something.

And nothing had really meant anything since her parents died.

Her eyes had welled with tears. Despite everything she'd been through, she hadn't cried in a long time.

It was strange to have her emotions coming back to life.

Matt took a deep breath and turned away. "I owe you one, for Terrence. I guess I'm sticking around to protect you from the bully this time. Spoiler alert: I'm pretty sure you're your own bully right now, Gems."

He'd walked out the door that night and left Gemma to deal with the outermost layer of her frozen shell thawing. That night, things had shifted between them. Something had stirred in Gemma. But she still had a long way to go before she hit rock bottom and decided to turn her life around. But Matt had come back that next morning, and the morning after, and the one after that. He'd never stopped coming back for her. Even after the job was done.

He'd never given up on her.

He'd saved her.

She snuggled up against him.

I may already be a little bit in love with you, Matt Silva, she thought, though she'd never say it out loud.

CHAPTER 3

"Fuck," Gemma said, pulling her pillow over her face. It'd only been a couple of hours since she closed her eyes, and she had no clue why she was awake at this ungodly hour.

A shrill sound assaulted her ears.

Oh. That's why.

Was it a fire alarm?

No, it was too musical… too…

Chimes.

It was chimes.

But not like the windchimes her great grandma used to have on her porch. Chimes like you'd hear from a game on someone's phone or…

The chimes stopped for a beautiful second.

Then they began again.

Louder, this time, if possible.

A ringtone, she thought. *It was a ringtone.*

She tried to move away from obnoxious noise but found herself pinned under the weight of Matt's large sleeping body. He lay on his side, pretzeled around her, his arm draped over her waist, one leg thrown across her hips and his calves clutching her ankles. The ringing stopped and almost immediately, started again.

She reached out to touch Matt's arm. His skin was warm like he'd slept outdoors on a beach and underneath the sun instead of in her small apartment. He was still asleep and wasn't budging.

She punched him lightly on the shoulder.

The chimes had stopped again and started *again*.

"Matt, your phone is ringing."

Matt jerked in his sleep and rolled over. He yanked the sheet with him, but he didn't wake up.

"Matt, your phone!" she said a little louder and, not for the first time since they'd been sleeping together, she cursed the fact that he was such a heavy sleeper.

Ding ding ding ding ding. Ding ding ding ding diiiiiiiiiiing.

"You deserve this, boy," she muttered quietly under her breath before giving him a hefty shove. Yes, he was quite a bit bigger than her. But she was stronger than your average girl her size. Matt landed on the floor with a loud thud.

"What the hell, Gems?" he asked groggily as he sat up and rubbed the back of his head.

She shot him a dirty look. "Your phone was ringing."

He blinked at her. His eyes only made it half open.

"My phone?" He yawned, trying to shake the sleep that still seemed to have a firm grip on him.

"Yeah. Your phone." She tried to mask just how irritated she really was. She was not a morning person. Or a middle-of-the-night person. A being-woken-abruptly-at-whatever-the-hell-time-it-was person. "Whoever it was called like four times."

Matt scrambled through the dark. "I can't find my pants. My phone's in my pocket."

"If I hear those annoying chimes again, I'm going to lose my—"

As if on cue: More chimes.

"Arrrrrrrrrgh."

"That's not my ringtone," Matt said. "So, you owe me an apology. And maybe an ass rub because your floors are hard and—"

"What do you mean it's not your ringtone?" she demanded, leaning over to flick on the lamp on the nightstand. Immediately regretting her decision, she squinted.

Lights bad.

"I believe that's your ringtone," he said, pointing toward the dresser where a black rectangle emitted a slight glow from underneath. He pulled his phone out of his back pants' pocket. Holding it up, he announced, triumphantly, "I turned my phone off earlier this evening."

"Well, who the hell would be calling me? Especially at this time of night?"

He shrugged as he climbed back into the bed and pulled the covers up. "I dunno, but you still owe me an ass rub."

Except for Matt and the typical telemarketer or a wrong number, no one *ever* called her cell.

"What time is it, anyway? It must be a wrong number. It's too late to ask about my Jeep's extended warranty. Plus, it's not like I'm on anyone's emergency contact list."

"For the love of God, Gems, just check. Maybe someone was trying to get a hold of me and figured I'm probably with you."

Gemma sighed and stole a glance at the dresser again. "Not everyone knows about us."

"Yeah, they do," Matt said. He huffed out a laugh. "Most of your customers and employees are all but certain we're sleeping together. They're just waiting for us to stop keeping it on the DL."

"We're just friends." She would always feel duty-bound to remind him.

He cocked an eyebrow. "Yeah. Friends who sleep together. Friends who give each other ass rubs…"

"I'm not rubbing your ass, Matthew," she said as she sat up and swung her legs off the side of the bed. She groaned.

"I'll settle for a—"

"No."

"Will you at least admit we're not *just* friends?"

"Please don't start this now, Matt. In case you hadn't noticed, I'm cranky."

His face fell into a frown, but he didn't say anything. They had this conversation every few weeks, and she wanted to believe that one day he would get over it. She couldn't tie herself to someone like that. Not after everything, everyone, she'd lost. Sleeping with him was one thing but making it some sort of official romantic relationship was something entirely different.

"Start what?" he began as he reached out and tried to pull her back into the bed. "Gems…"

She knew what he wanted to say. He wanted more. She didn't. They always wound up at an impasse, with her suggesting they stop sleeping together so he could find someone who wanted the same things he did and him saying he didn't want that.

This time, Gemma took the phone as an easy out. Quickly pulling out of his grip, she started fumbling with the items on top of her dresser.

"Okay, let's see who just couldn't wait until the morning to call me."

Gemma looked at the number. Then the name attached to the number. The screen was blurred as her hands shook. "It can't be."

"What is it?"

Gemma blinked. "It was my sister. It was Danielle."

Matt quickly got up and strode across the room, placing a comforting hand on her shoulder. "You never talk about your sister."

She stepped back, shrugging away from his touch. "Yeah. Because she isn't a part of my life."

She swallowed hard, her throat burning with unshed tears.

As long as she pretended Dani simply didn't exist, she could keep the pain at bay. But Dani had called her. Dani had reached out. Dani…

According to the notification on her phone, Dani had left a voicemail.

Overwhelmed, Gemma paced the small apartment while she clutched her phone tightly.

"But she *could* be. Dani got married and moved to start a new life for herself with her husband, Gems. It happens," Matt said as he stopped her in her tracks by holding her shoulders. "It doesn't mean she—"

"A new life that had no room for me in it, Matt. With her *husband*," Gemma scoffed. Danielle had barely even known Clay when he proposed. "They could have gotten a place in East Haven and stayed close, but *he* didn't want that. He wanted to move all the way to fucking Harmony Springs. And she chose him over me."

She said *Harmony Springs* as if she was saying the *seventh circle of Hell*.

Matt lowered his head and tried to look into her eyes, but she turned away. She knew she sounded like a toddler throwing a tantrum.

Danielle and Clay had made their home in a house Gemma and Danielle's parents purchased in secret at some point before their deaths. A house they'd left only Danielle in their will. Gemma couldn't even tell Matt that without sounding petty and jealous, like an entitled niece who didn't get grandma's prized emerald earrings. Especially since she hadn't exactly been left out of the will herself. She had the Moonlight because of the money her parents had left her.

"Gemma, maybe you should just hear what she—"

"Whose side are you on, anyway?" Gemma snapped, cutting him off. She sounded so much like mean drunk Gemma again. She hated herself for taking all her pent-up negative feelings out on Matt.

"You know I'm looking at things from *all* sides," he said reasonably.

A journalist to his core, Matt prided himself at being impartial. He wanted the truth and nothing but. His own opinions were secondary.

But there was so much to this story Matt didn't know. Gemma'd never even told him outright that Dani had cut her off completely. She'd already said too much, not only shown him that the wound was still very much open but infected as well.

"You said it was her choice to leave. Now it's your choice whether to let her back in, if that's what she wants," he said softly. "Take some time to think about it. Then call her back if—and when—you decide you're ready—"

"She left a message."

"Oh," Matt said. "Do you… want to listen to it? Do you want me to stick around for moral support or… Would you prefer I give you some privacy?"

Gemma's knuckles paled where she was holding onto her phone for dear life. It was starting to feel like a twenty-pound weight. She looked at Matt with unshed tears in her eyes.

She nodded. Walking back to the bed, she sat with the

phone cradled in both of her hands, Gemma quietly said, "This is something I need to do alone, I think."

Just as Randy showing up tonight hadn't been a coincidence, Danielle calling tonight of all nights couldn't be one, either.

And just like she'd had to keep the conversation with Randy tightly reined in while Matt was present, letting him hear even one side of a conversation with Danielle might result in him learning things he most certainly did not need to be aware of.

"Do you want me to spend the rest of the night at my place?" he asked.

"Would you mind?" she asked, already knowing what the answer would be.

Though he wouldn't want to go, he would give her what she needed.

He brushed his lips across her cheek and went to his side of the bed, picking his pants back up and pulling them on. "If you need me, call."

"Okay." It didn't feel okay, but she said it anyway.

He stopped at the door and turned around. "You promise me?"

He had her and he knew it. Gemma had never broken a promise to him.

"I promise I will call you if I need you," she said, with an emphasis on the *if*.

"You don't always have to be tough, you know."

"I know that," she said. But did she? She wasn't sure. "And it's not like I don't appreciate you." That was true. "I really do, Matt. But there are some things I prefer to do alone. I need you to understand that."

Knowing that was all he was going to get from her, Matt kissed the top of her head before heading out the door. Hearing him lock it behind him, Gemma stared at the phone, paralyzed with trepidation. Once she listened Danielle's voicemail, everything would change. One way or another. Her sister had been clear when she left that she was leaving everything in East Haven behind, including Gemma. Despite Matt's optimism, there had been no ambiguity about that. Even just dialing Gemma's number meant something, somewhere had already changed.

It's your choice, Matt had said.

And it was her choice.

Gemma knew she was being spiteful and maybe even a coward, but in that moment, she chose to power off her phone. She got back into bed, determined to fall back asleep, determined not to think about the bottle of Absinthe.

After a few hours of tossing and turning, she gave up on both.

Without letting herself overthink it, she turned her phone back on, put it on speaker, and played the message.

"Gemma? Gemma? Are you there?"

She gasped.

The voice was muffled and a bit distorted, but it really was Danielle. Her sister's voice trembled as if she was trying hard not to cry. And the fear, there was so much fear in her words. Panic infiltrated every syllable.

Gemma's heart clenched like an angry fist. The small hairs on the back of her neck stood at attention. Goose-bumps arose on her arms. Something was wrong.

Danielle wasn't just calling because it was the anniversary of their parents' death and she got sad and missed her only living relative. Her sister.

"Gemma, please call me back," Danielle begged. "I need your help. It's bad. Real bad."

Her problems are not your problems anymore, Gemma reminded herself.

But she took a shaky deep breath in. Letting it out slowly, she steeled herself for the call. The dread was pervasive, but she tried to summon every bit of training she had on staying clearheaded during a crisis. Danielle would only call if there was no other option. In case of an emergency. And in that instant, even if it was because Danielle didn't have a choice, the five painful years apart didn't matter. Gemma would be there for her sister, no matter what.

Danielle's problems would always be her problems.

Hitting redial, Gemma wasn't surprised Danielle answered on the first ring.

"Gemma," Danielle sounded as if she'd been holding her breath, waiting on Gemma to call back. "Thank God! I was afraid maybe you had changed your number."

There were plenty of times Gemma thought about changing her number, purely out of spite. In case this day ever came. In case Dani ever needed her then, oops, too bad. But she never believed this day *would* come. Well, maybe, somewhere in the farthest recesses of her mind, where she stuffed hope into a cramped corner with other useless feelings.

"Gemma?" Danielle asked. "Are you there?"

The joy that Gemma felt at hearing her sister say her name was quickly replaced by concern as she remembered why she'd placed the call.

"What's going on, Dani?"

God, how she longed to hug her again. To see her face.

"*Dani.* I missed hearing that," her sister said, letting out a small chuckle. "No one calls me that anymore."

I miss saying it, Gemma thought to herself, already getting lost in the sea of emotions, her attention drifting again from the fact that Danielle had called for a reason. A *bad* reason.

"I need your help." The simple sentence was followed by a series of unintelligible sobs intermingled with a word or two here and there. Finally, she managed to choke out, "It's Clay."

Gemma could feel her blood pressure rising.

"What?" she demanded. "Did he hit you? I'll kill that son of a…" Gemma glanced around the room, quickly searching for her shoes, keys, and wallet. She was ready to head out right this second if she needed to deliver some swift and effective justice.

She'd known he was bad news from the moment she found out her sister was romantically involved with him.

"No, no," Dani said. "He would never, Gemma! Clay was attacked!"

The admission was rushed. Dani's voice high and frantic. As if Clay were still actively in danger.

Taking a deep breath, Gemma calmly said, "I'm not following. Isn't that something the local police force should handle?"

Gemma feared she knew the answer to her question before she even asked it, but she wanted to hear what Danielle had to say. She wanted to live in plausible deniability for just a moment longer, wanted their past to stay in the past.

"Gemma, the local police force is not equipped to handle something like this." Danielle's voice was tight. There was so much her tone said that her words did not. Gemma's body became fully alert. At that moment, she knew she wasn't going to like the answer.

"Danielle, what attacked Clay?" Gemma asked.

Fear filled her lungs like a bucket of lead, stopping her from taking another breath. She had no idea what the answer would be, but she knew it wouldn't be a burglar or a mugger or a random act of violence by a gang of unruly teenagers.

And this was why Gemma didn't want to have unfiltered conversations with Randy around Matt. Why she didn't want to have conversations with Danielle around Matt. Because he didn't know she came from a long line of Hunters. Hell, he didn't even know this kind of Hunter existed. Randy and the Jaegers, they weren't the type of hunters who killed deer to fill their freezers with venison meat. They weren't the type of heartless wealthy hunters who flew to other countries to gun down exotic animals for a photo op. They didn't duck hunt or squirrel hunt or fox hunt.

No. They hunted the preternatural.

"A Fury, Gemma," Danielle whispered. "Clay was attacked by a Fury."

Gemma's vision blurred as the phone dropped to the floor.

Gemma stared at it for a long moment before picking it back up.

She *had* to have heard Danielle wrong.

"Did you say," Gemma began, then lowered her voice. "A *Fury?*"

"Yes." Danielle's response, too, was hushed.

Even though her sister couldn't see her, Gemma shook her head.

"Gemma. Are you still there?" Dani asked.

"Yeah, I'm here," she said. She was trying to summon some words to comfort Dani, who, despite the estrangement, would always be her sister. But unfortunately, the words that came out were, "So you're calling because you need me to help you dispose of the body?"

Danielle gasped, horrified, as if she'd forgotten *that* part of being a Hunter. But if Clay had truly been killed by a

Fury, it's not like Danielle could just call 911 and get the small-town coroner to come do his job as if it were a normal crime scene. She couldn't risk getting the authorities involved. There would be too many questions she couldn't answer without winding up under in-patient psychiatric care again or, worse, on trial for murder.

"Gemma!" Danielle admonished. Through clenched teeth, Gemma could tell. "Clay is not dead! He's in the hospital, fighting for his life. And he *is* going to make it. I know you can't stand him, but I'd appreciate it if you would not be so callous, for my sake."

You didn't do anything for my *sake, Danielle,* Gemma thought. There wasn't a 12-step program for addiction to bitterness, as far as she knew.

"Then it couldn't be a Fury that attacked him. Furies are vicious killers, Danielle. You know that. They're unmerciful. They don't leave victims alive. Ever."

"Don't you think I know that?" Danielle nearly yelled. "But this one *did*." She sniffled. "It left Clay alive. Barely."

Not possible.

"Our neighbor heard a commotion and ran outside. The Fury was already gone, and Clay was unconscious."

"Where were you?" Gemma made a conscious effort to soften the question so it couldn't be mistaken as an accusation. Danielle would already be beating herself up. She didn't need anyone else—least of all the only person she could call for help—piling on.

"I was in the house. I must've fallen asleep," Danielle's voice quivered. "I didn't hear anything, until the sirens of the ambulance. I realized he wasn't inside and I got worried, so I ran out to see what was happening."

Why didn't the neighbor come and get Danielle as soon as they found Clay?

"He's in surgery now."

Gemma hadn't heard Danielle sound so scared and helpless since the night they lost their parents.

"What do you need me to do, Dani? Just say the word." Gemma hadn't realized until that moment that an unacknowledged part of her had been yearning for this call since the day Dani left. Of course, she wished it would've come under better circumstances, but couldn't deny the longing she felt for the chance to be a big sister again, nonetheless.

"Can you come here? To Harmony Springs?" Danielle asked. "I need to be with Clay, to protect him, but the Fury *must* be found before it attacks again. You know it'll come back to finish what it started. But I can't be in two places at once, so…"

Gemma yelped as if she'd been punched.

Danielle didn't want her sister. She wanted a skilled Hunter and her sister happened to be one. Danielle probably didn't care if she even got to see Gemma while she was in Harmony Springs, as long as Gemma dispatched the damn Fury and kept her precious Clay from being on the receiving end of another attack.

"I know you're not Clay's biggest fan. I get you don't want to do this for him. But can you put your feelings about him aside and do this for me?" Danielle pleaded. "Gemma, there's no one else I can call."

Gemma hesitated.

She *should* be happy her baby sister needed her help, but all she felt was the sting of rejection once again. By Danielle's own admission, Danielle had only called because there was *no one else she could call*. As if calling Gemma wouldn't have ever crossed Dani's mind otherwise. It was as if they'd never been close. As if their bond hadn't only been broken but forgotten altogether.

"Please. For me. This is my husband's *life* that I am

asking you to help me protect. I can't lose him," Danielle sobbed. "Haven't I lost enough?"

Gemma drew in a breath and exhaled slowly. She cleared her throat.

"We've both lost enough, Danielle," she said, sadly.

But we never had to lose each other.

And now, no matter why Dani had called, she had called.

This was a chance to maybe rebuild the bridge Dani had burned… or to spit in its ashes.

Gemma listened to her sister cry. She bit her bottom lip until blood beaded around her teeth. Tamping down all her own emotions bubbling to the surface, she focused on what Danielle must be feeling. She was alone and she needed someone. Gemma could identify with that.

Because she left you! You're alone because she left you! Let her suffer! Let her know what it feels like to have no one!

Gemma pushed away the selfish thoughts.

Being a big sister meant taking care of your family, even when it was hard. Even when it hurt like hell. Even when it shouldn't be your responsibility any longer.

"Never mind," Danielle snapped, breaking Gemma's thoughtful silence. "I'll figure something out. Forget I—"

"No!" Gemma blurted. "I'm coming." She glanced at the time. "I'll be there by noon."

"Oh, thank God," Danielle said. "Thank you. Thank you, thank you. And Gemma?"

"Gemma?"

"Yeah?"

"I love you."

The words sent her heartbeat into overdrive. It had been so long since she heard them from anyone. "Go check on Clay. And don't worry; I'll take care of everything."

She sounded so self-assured, so confident, but the

moment she ended the call, she was engulfed by pure terror. Her hands shook, no, they *flapped*. Flapped like the wings of a frantic bird who couldn't take flight. Her legs felt like the blood in their veins had turned to lead. Was she breathing? It was like she had no control over her body. She sat down on the edge of her bed.

What was she so afraid of?

She shook her head.

The first thing she needed to do was to get as clear-headed as possible.

A cold shower did the trick. With the icy water assaulting her skin like a spray of frozen needles, all thoughts were driven from her mind. She emerged sharp and alert. She got dressed quickly.

Then she went into the former supply room that had been converted into a vast walk-in closet. But unlike most women's closets, hers wasn't filled with clothes and shoes. Her small, functional wardrobe fit in her dresser. Ignoring all the boxes that lined the side walls, she strode to the large trunk pushed against the very back exposed brick wall. She hadn't planned on ever having to open that trunk again, but with a resigned sigh, she located the key where she'd tucked it in an otherwise empty jewelry box on the highest shelf.

A fucking Fury.

She took long, ragged breaths while she slid down to sit on the floor in front of the trunk. She unlocked it and edged the lid open. With a creak, the brittle, worn leather and dark wood flecked with silver lifted to reveal its contents. Each individual object had been carefully wrapped in cloth and stacked neatly.

Weapons.

Some three hundred years old, or more. Swords, Bowie knives, daggers. Firearms. You know it, she had it. Even a

Kukri—a blade used by the Gurkhas of Nepal for bravery and honor.

The Kukri had been passed down from her great-great-Aunt Seble Zemichael Jaeger, along with the story about how she'd used it to single-handedly destroy an entire pack of hellhounds terrorizing a western town in the 1800s.

Aunt Seble was an OG badass, Gemma thought, idly, as she moved the Kukri aside to find the crossbow given to her by her father when she turned 14. Back then, *what do you want to be when you grow up?* hadn't even been a question. She'd be a badass, too. Teenaged Gemma hadn't even questioned whether she had a choice. She hadn't realized not being a Hunter was an option until she'd walked away from the life.

Every weapon had a specific purpose, meaning, and history. Every weapon had been used to kill and kill again. They were artifacts of the life she, and so many relatives before her, had lived. Testaments to the violence they'd been a part of and witnessed. To both the victories they'd basked in and the losses they'd endured.

Gemma packed as quickly as possible, the urgency to get to Danielle growing with every passing moment.

The gnawing fear growing, too, senseless and raging like a wildfire.

A fucking Fury, Gemma thought again.

But why was she so terrified?

Maybe she wasn't a born badass like Aunt Seble, but still. She'd faced far worse than Furies.

Since Drew would likely be hungover, she called Leslie, one of her other bartenders, and asked her to manage the place while she was gone. Then she called Matt—thankfully getting his voicemail—and left a quick message for him.

Then Gemma dashed out to her Jeep. Her extra-large

duffel bag of clothes and weapons went behind the passenger's seat. Two bottles of water went in the console up front. Then she slid in behind the steering wheel. Once she hit the highway, she didn't plan on stopping until she got to Danielle. And Harmony Springs.

With each mile came more questions. Furies didn't just show up in random places. They didn't attack random people. When Furies came, they came with a purpose, a specific intent, and—at least in their minds—a deserving target. The wrath of a Fury was always fueled by a personal vengeance. They didn't just attack for shits and giggles.

And that, Gemma realized, was the source of her terror.

What if the Fury's intended victim hadn't been Clay at all?

A Fury going after Danielle would make sense, after all. Both Gemma and her sister had the blood of so many creatures on their hands. They'd each made many kills in their young lives. It wouldn't be out of the realm of possibility a Fury to seek one of them out, looking for revenge. But the supposed Fury hadn't attacked Dani.

Why would a Fury come for Clay?

Was it possible he was involved with the preternatural somehow? That he'd made his own non-human enemies?

Gemma doubted it. She hadn't gotten any Hunter vibes from him. Hell, she doubted Danielle ever even told him about their family. And why would she?

She just let him whisk her away to Happily Ever After without glancing back. She left it all behind.

The blacktop stretched on as Gemma lost herself to the questions. Clay had to have the answer, but would he be willing to share it with her? Would he even want to talk to her? She didn't have time to worry about that. Gemma had to help her sister. Regardless of how Clay felt about her or vice versa. This was about Dani now.

This would have been the time she'd have gone to their mother for advice. They would sit down and weigh the options and come up with a solution.

But that wasn't an option anymore.

Her grief for her mother brought her thoughts back around to last night when Randy strode through the doors of her bar and back into her life. He had offered his help if she ever needed it. And, God, did she need it now.

As soon as she got settled in and knew what she was looking at, she would ask Randy what he thought. Having another Hunter's perspective would be invaluable. Now that she had a game plan, Gemma cranked up the seventies station and drove on.

CHAPTER 4

With each glimpse at the rearview mirror, the dreary clouds seemed to swallow up more of the tall buildings as Gemma left the city of East Haven behind.

To go to fucking Harmony Springs.

With the thought came the rain, which splattered against the windshield in fat drops.

The sky darkened ahead of her, foreboding.

Turn around, it seemed to say. *Worse weather ahead.*

It should be Danielle coming home to East Haven, not Gemma going to Harmony Springs. A place neither of them belonged.

Why had her parents bought a house there, and left it to Danielle?

It was a question that would never be answered. A question that would plague her forever. She wished it was the only one.

Gemma set the cruise control and settled in for a long drive. It would be miles before another exit would pop up on the highway that led out of the state.

Harmony Springs was almost 300 miles away.

There was a time Gemma liked to drive alone. Loved it, even. It gave her time to think. But now her thoughts were an army of enemies. Hard to defeat. Easier to just turn away, pretend they weren't there, and hope they decided to retreat instead of attack.

She yawned. Cranking up the radio station, she hoped it would keep her awake. She cranked it more, until it was too loud for thinking to even be a possibility. Just as she was about to belt out the solo to one of her favorite songs, the music was muted for a call.

A call from Matt.

She took a deep breath and answered.

"Sorry I missed you earlier." His apology was both immediate and sincere.

Of course, he'd call back. He was Matt.

She'd hoped he would just check his voicemail, be satisfied with the message she'd left, and leave it at that. She didn't want to have to lie to him, and if he kept asking questions, she would have no choice.

"It's fine. I was just letting you know what was going on so you wouldn't worry," she said.

"Are you going to be okay up there?" His voice was laden with concern, as if it had been Gemma who'd been attacked, and not the brother-in-law she disliked. "Harmony Springs is way out in the country, right?"

"Yes," she replied. "But I'm sure this city girl can hack being in a Podunk town for a night or two. It's not like I'm going to be camping in the woods. And I promise I'll avoid any shady looking hillbillies."

She'd been trying to make him laugh, but he only sighed.

"Matt, I promise. I'll be fine." Now she sighed. "This has been a long time coming."

It took him a second to respond, and when he did, he sounded confused. "Your brother-in-law being attacked has been a long time coming?"

"No." She heard the frustration in her own voice and

tried to tamp it down. She couldn't expect Matt to understand when he only knew bits and pieces of her past. Truth be told, she wasn't even thinking about the Clay aspect of this trip. Whatever happened to him—it wasn't something that required a Huntress. The more she thought about it, the more she believed Danielle had to have been wrong. It couldn't have been a Fury. Furies were so rare. East Haven, where she and Danielle had been born and raised, was a hotbed of preternatural activity. That's why so many Hunters lived there. Yet no one in their family had ever encountered one in real life or knew of any other Hunter who had. Whatever happened to Clay, it was a matter for the Harmony Springs police. She was sure of that.

But the call to come to Harmony Springs was a means to an end. A reason to see Danielle again. Pulling one hand off the steering wheel, she wiped her hand over her face as if she were swiping away unwanted emotions. "I meant me seeing my sister. It's something I should have done sooner."

Somehow, over the past few years, she'd tricked herself into thinking she could spend the rest of her life pretending Danielle didn't exist. If she didn't acknowledge the pain, it would go away. But now she realized what a foolish pursuit that had been.

"Okay." Matt paused for a long minute. She felt her eyelids growing heavy. "As long as you're okay." Another pause. She forced her eyes open wide. "Are you okay?"

"Yes. I'm fine."

"So... you said your brother-in-law was in an accident. Like an automobile accident?"

"I don't know all the details," she said, which was true. She couldn't elaborate. She'd only heard Danielle's speculations, and that wasn't something she could share.

"Because I searched online and there's no mention of

any car crashes or any incidents with injuries in or near Harmony Springs recently. In fact, it's weird, Gems, but I can't find any news about Harmony Springs. Like... any."

"That is weird," Gemma agreed. "But it is a hick town. Their newspaper probably comes out once a week if they have one at all. And I bet it's definitely not online."

"Maybe," Matt mused. "Do you know how serious Clay's injuries are?"

"I really don't know anything, Matt," she said, trying—and failing miserably—not to sound snippy. "Sorry. I'm just upset. Worried about Danielle."

"And Clay," Matt prompted, because that's what a good person would say. He thought of Gemma as a good person, despite everything.

"And Clay," she echoed, though there wasn't much truth to it.

Sure, she wanted Clay to be okay, for Danielle's sake.

But if Clay wasn't okay, maybe Danielle would come back to East Haven. Maybe she'd…

Alright, not *what a good person would think,* Gemma chastised herself.

"I get it. I'll let you go. Unless you want me to stay on the line with you for the drive, keep you company?"

"No!" Gemma cried, then she said, softer, "No. I'm not feeling very talkative." She expected him to argue. To say that when she didn't feel very talkative was when she needed to talk the most. She hastily added, "Plus, you've got work to do."

"Oh, yes, very important work. I've got to go interview residents of the Emerald Hills neighborhood about their new HOA policies. Garden flags are now forbidden. Apparently, there's a public outcry," Matt said, sarcastically.

She'd heard—a lot—about how desperate he was to be

assigned a real story. *This isn't journalism. It's ridiculous puff pieces strung together by the occasional article worthy of being called news.* Sometimes she found herself worried that he'd become so dissatisfied with his career, he'd move to a major city, like Detroit or Chicago or New York.

East Haven is a lot of things, he'd said occasionally, with a resigned sigh. But *The City That Never Sleeps* it's not.

Oh, Matt, if only you knew, she'd think.

East Haven didn't have the nightlife of NYC, but it had an altogether different kind of scene after dark. And some-times—if you wound up in the wrong place at the wrong time—in broad daylight, too.

"Anyway," he said, breaking into her thoughts. "Call me later? Keep me updated?"

"Of course. Talk to you later," she said. She quickly hung before he could come up with more questions to ask her.

Her music resumed, and she drove on.

Matt hadn't asked her to keep him updated as an idle pleasantry. He'd expect her to check in regularly. She'd have to keep those check-ins vague. He knew so little about this other side of her life, about the years between when she knew him as a boy and when they reconnected as adults. Sometimes the secrets felt like a dark shadow standing in front of her soul. Part of her yearned to tell him everything, but Matt was so inquisitive. The more she told him, the more he'd want to know. And the more he knew, the more danger he'd inevitably find himself in.

She'd have to figure out a way to keep him informed of the situation without actually informing him of anything at all. But she had a while before she had to figure out the logistics. For now, she just wanted to concentrate on the drive and let all the other stuff fall to the wayside until it had to be dealt with.

I'll figure out how to cross those bridges when I roll up on them, she thought.

Getting to Harmony Springs seemed to take forever—she wanted to see Danielle so badly she felt like waiting another second would kill her. But the trip also seemed to happen too fast—she'd never been to Harmony Springs, but that didn't stop her from hating it with every fiber of her being.

The small town was well-kept with mostly one-story buildings in various shades of beige and grey. To Gemma, something about it she couldn't quite put her finger on made it seem more like a movie set of a small town than an actual small town. Everything looked brand new, but that wasn't it.

The flowers, she realized.

Bushes dotted with pastel blooms were everywhere, even though it wasn't spring.

They had to be fake.

Gemma rolled down her window and inhaled deeply. The sweet and heady floral scent that filled her nostrils smelled real.

And the temperature!

It was that almost unachievable *just right* between cool and warm.

The sun peeked out behind the streaks of pure white clouds, like cotton stretched out across a watercolor blue sky.

Despite the nice day there was hardly any traffic.

Gemma stopped at a crosswalk to let an older couple stroll across the street. They stared at her car as they passed in front of it, both squinting as to see if they recognized the driver.

They probably don't get many visitors here, Gemma realized.

After a long moment, they both raised their hands in

unison, as if the friendly small-town wave had been chore-ographed.

Hitting the navigation app, Gemma drove slowly while it recalculated. The posted speed limit was mind-blowingly slow twenty-five miles an hour, but Gemma crept along, making sure not to go above it. She was not about to take a chance of getting pulled with the small arsenal weapons in the back of her Jeep. Fortunately, she didn't go far before Danielle's house was pinned on the map. It didn't take long to get to her final destination: A decent-sized Tudor-style house that made her blood hot in her veins.

But Gemma couldn't let herself think about the house's back story now.

The home—Danielle's home with *Clay*—wasn't huge by any means, but it must have three, maybe four bedrooms. Enough room for a nursery or—

Gemma gasped.

Enough time had passed since she'd last spoken to Danielle, she could have a niece or a nephew. A niece and a nephew.

As she pulled into the driveway, Gemma surveyed the yard for any tell-tale signs of children but came up empty. The front door was a cheery red with a wreath made of sunflowers hung over the peephole. The brass doorknob gleamed as if someone came by to polish it several times a day. She parked next to a two-seater convertible—the same kind of car Clay had back in East Haven, just in a newer model.

Before Gemma could take anything else in, a voice pierced the silence.

"Gemma!"

Danielle bounded towards her. Before Gemma was even all the way out of the Jeep, her baby sister enveloped her in a hug.

"You made it!" Danielle cried, holding her tight. "You don't know how much this means to me."

A huge lump formed in Gemma's throat as she fought back tears, which defiantly welled up in her eyes anyway. She untangled herself from Danielle's embrace.

Don't get too comfortable, she told herself.

For all she knew, in Danielle's mind, Gemma was just here for a case and once that case was closed, Danielle would turn her away again.

Gemma took a step back and studied her sister through blurry eyes.

Danielle hadn't changed.

She had the same curls as Gemma, but she still wore hers short.

Excuse me, but I'm not going to give a zombie a ponytail or handful of braids to hold my head still while they eat my brains, she'd always said. *But you do you, Gemmie.*

For the record: They'd never encountered a zombie.

Dani still wore white Keds, faded jeans, and a quirky t-shirt. Today's featured a big-eyed bumblebee with the phrase *Bee Well* underneath it in cursive. They'd always varied from positive, upbeat messages to sarcastic puns, depending on Dani's mood. Apparently, this one was a wish for Clay.

"I know you won't believe this, but I have missed you so much." Danielle's cheeks were wet. She wiped at her eyes.

Are those tears for me or Clay, though?

"You have?" Gemma had intended to ask the question with pleasant surprise in her voice, but it landed between them with a thud of doubt.

"Of course." Dani tilted her head. She stared at Gemma as if she had three eyes. "I wanted to call you so, so often, but I felt you didn't want to hear from me with the way we left things."

I think you mean with the way you *left things, sis.*

Gemma swallowed the bitter words, finding that they literally left a bad taste in her mouth.

"That's not important right now," Gemma said, going back to the Jeep for her bags. "Why aren't you at the hospital? You made it sound like you weren't going to leave Clay's side."

Danielle flinched. Pain and remorse flashed across her features.

She *hadn't* wanted to leave Clay's side.

"I wanted to be here to let you in the house and help you get settled in. I wasn't going to let you wait in the driveway until I got home."

Even though Dani didn't make it sound like Gemma's arrival was an inconvenience, Gemma couldn't help but wonder if she felt that way, deep down. Had she really wanted to call Gemma so, so often?

Gemma scanned the immediate area. "Well... I could've used the extra key hidden inside the blue flowerpot to let myself in?"

A smile grew on her sister's face. "You still know me so well."

Gemma shrugged, as if it was no big deal.

"Blue has been your favorite color since we were children," Gemma answered. "It wasn't that hard to figure out."

"Hello! Hello!" a jolly voice rang out.

Gemma quickly turned to see an elderly woman hobbling up the sidewalk towards them. Hunched over, she walked with a cane. With her free hand, she waved; the gesture eerily similar to the way the couple had waved at

Gemma when she was driving into town. Did they practice it at town meetings?

"Ohh, crap!" Dani blurted. Then she whispered in a rush to Gemma. "We use the last name Smith now, not Hickman."

What the…

"Hello, darling!" the woman greeted Danielle as she approached them. She walked right past Gemma, almost stepping on her toes.

"Miss Coffey!" Even though the woman was less than a foot away from her, Danielle spoke extra loudly, taking obvious care to enunciate each syllable, as if she knew the woman had hearing issues. "How are you doing?"

Maybe she can't see well, either, Gemma mused.

"On edge, dear. Very on edge. But it's going to be alright, I know it!"

"I hope so, Miss Coffey," Dani said. She walked around the older woman, and over to Gemma. Putting her arm around Gemma, Dani said, "Miss Coffey, this is my sister, Gemma Jaeger. Gemma, this is my neighbor, Miss Coffey. She lives across the street."

Miss Coffey turned to face Gemma.

She looked Gemma up and down.

Was the woman squinting at the sun or giving her the stink eye? Gemma wasn't sure.

Standing half a foot shorter than Gemma, the woman's fair skin wasn't much darker than her stark white hair. She wore a thin pair of shorts, a loose t-shirt, and beach sandals. All of which should have given her a laid-back appearance, but her lemon-puckered face ruined the effect.

"Oh, you have company," Miss Coffey said. She pronounced company as if it were three separate words, none of which she particularly cared for.

Gemma couldn't put her finger on it, but there was

something about Miss Coffey that unsettled her. Her bony fingers clenched her knotted walking stick like she was ready to yank it up and swing it like a weapon any second. Her weathered skin was lined with age spots, but her eyes were as shrewd and clear as a cat's. An unusual shade of gray, they bored into Gemma. Miss Coffey was a tiny wisp of a woman, but there was serious fight in her stare.

"Hello, young lady," she said, her face smoothing into a pleasant expression. "I've told your sister time and time again to call me Addie. She's a fantastic neighbor, your sister. As I was telling her, Clay's attack has all of us on edge. Most people are scared to leave their home." Gemma looked down the street and saw no movement. Miss Coffey went on, "Did she tell you it was some kind of wild cat that did it? Maybe a mountain lion! Or was it a cougar? Either way, I am certain everything will be just fine."

Gemma glanced at Danielle out of the corner of her eye.

"The lead Fish and Wildlife Service agent is on it," Danielle piped up quickly. "I'm sure they'll catch whatever it was soon."

"Agent Palmer is very good at his job," Miss Coffey nodded. Did her voice sound defensive? She went on, "I didn't know our Danielle had a sister."

Miss Coffey said it politely, casually. But it stung as if it was a poison arrow precisely and intentionally aimed at Gemma's weakest of spots. "Odd time for you to be visiting, maybe?"

"Addie," Dani said, with a definite edge to her voice. "This is a difficult time and Gemma's come to support me through it. Though I do wish she'd visited under better circumstances, I'm very glad she's here."

Did Danielle legitimately feel that way or was she just

putting on a *we're one big happy family* show for the nosy neighbor?

Gemma wished she could just take everything her sister said and did at face value. Assume that her words and actions were genuine.

"And how long do you think she'll be here?" Miss Coffey asked Dani and only Dani, as if Gemma wasn't, in fact, there at all.

Gemma cleared her throat. "Our plans are open-ended," she said firmly before Dani could answer.

Miss Coffey's wizened eyes narrowed on Gemma. Almost imperceptibly, she raised an eyebrow.

"Then I'll leave you two to it." With a lift of her chin, Ms. Coffey turned her attention back to Dani. "Are you planning on heading back to the hospital soon, Danielle? I'm sure Clay appreciates you being there, by his side."

Now Gemma raised an eyebrow—not imperceptibly at all—at the old lady. She seemed to have a lot of nerve. Danielle put a hand on Gemma's arm, giving it a gentle squeeze right below her elbow. Their old signal. *It's okay*, she said, without speaking the words.

"Yes, as soon as my sister is settled in, I'll be headed back to the hospital," Danielle said with a smile. She turned herself and Gemma around, calling over her shoulder, "Have a good day, Miss Coffey."

"Addie!"

"Right. Have a good day, Addie!"

"You, too, dear. And it was very nice to meet you, Jenna!"

"The pleasure was all mine," Gemma said through clenched teeth. She glanced over her shoulder.

"Same to you," Gemma said, straining her neck around to look at Miss Coffey who didn't make a move to walk away. She just stood on the sidewalk waving that creepy wave; a fake grin plastered on her face.

When the sisters reached the front door, they turned and watched as the elderly woman finally decided to walk away.

"Your neighbor seems… nice." Gemma'd hoped the comment came off light and casual, though she felt the opposite. Something was odd about that woman, and Danielle should recognize it. They were both trained to never overlook something off-kilter or out of place.

Deep down in her gut, Gemma felt like she was being assessed by Miss Coffey, almost as if to determine whether or not she was going to be trouble.

Shrugging her shoulders, Danielle replied, "Well, she's a widow. And she's a busybody. She's harmless, though."

Gemma gathered her things, making sure she'd left nothing in the Jeep before locking it with the remote. She followed Danielle inside the front door.

"I got the feeling she wasn't very happy I'm here," Gemma said, unable to let it go even though she knew she probably should. She didn't want her sister to feel like she was judging her neighbors already. To give Dani any reason to regret asking her to come already.

"Well, we all kind of look out for one another, one of the perks of small-town life." Danielle shut the door behind them. She turned the deadbolt, ending the illusion that there still existed idyllic small towns where people didn't lock their doors… despite who was looking out for them.

"Well, if you ask me, Harmony Springs is a little bit too small," Gemma said before silently kicking herself. Was *this* how she wanted her first interaction with Danielle in so many years to go? Starting a fight with her over absolutely nothing?

Perhaps Miss Coffey was simply a harmless widow and other than being a busybody, she was a perfectly lovely person. Perhaps the problem was Gemma's perception. She was predisposed to dislike anyone who was in Dani's life now, because they *were* in Dani's life, where she hadn't been allowed. She had to admit, even if Miss Coffey had been perfectly lovely, the nicest person ever, she'd likely feel at least a little resentment that this total stranger was closer now to Dani than she was, knew more about her life now, who she was now.

"You get used to the slow pace," Dani said. "To everybody wanting to know your business."

Not likely, Gemma thought to herself, following Danielle through the living room and into the kitchen. She hadn't even gotten used to Matt wanting to know her business.

"Clay and I are the youngest couple in this town. Most Harmony Springs residents have been here all their lives. Born here, raised here, never left."

"And you don't find that weird?" Gemma cocked an eyebrow.

"It's just a tranquil place to grow old. I think that's why Mom and Dad bought this house. They'd planned to retire here. I think they were just waiting for us to go out on our own."

Gemma gulped down whatever bitter thing she'd spew if she spoke.

She could not picture her mom and dad in Harmony Springs. She could not picture them ever retiring, and it wasn't just because they'd never got the opportunity to. This town... Even if they'd made it to 95, her parents would've climbed the walls here. Her dad would've said tranquil was a synonym for dull.

"I noticed as I pulled up that the house actually backs up to the woods," Gemma said, trying not to laugh at the image of her mom sitting on the porch with Miss Coffey, crocheting in rocking chairs, or her dad in a boat on a nearby pond, patiently waiting for a fish to bite.

Stop it, Gemma told herself.

Had Danielle never met Clay... Had Danielle told Gemma she wanted Gemma to move to Harmony Springs with her instead, Gemma would've packed up without hesitation. She herself would've quite happily loved to crochet and sit on the rocking chairs on Miss Coffey's porch with her.

She'd never admit it out loud, but she knew she would have. She would sign up for a roach-infested condo in hell if Dani was with her.

But Dani hadn't wanted to have anything to do with Harmony Springs, or this house, until Clay had convinced her otherwise.

"Yes, it backs up to the woods, and then there are the mountains beyond," Danielle said as she opened the back door. Beyond the screen door, the tree line was evident less than three hundred feet away from the small back patio. "I think that's how it got away without being seen if I am being honest. I always liked the privacy of being so close to the forest, but now it just seems like a nightmare."

"By *it* you mean... the Fury?" Gemma lowered her voice.

Dani shuddered but nodded.

Closing the door, she walked Gemma back through the living room and to the mouth of a hallway.

Gemma surveyed the living room more closely this time. The oversized furniture made it look even smaller than it was, but it was what was missing, not what was there, that clued her in on some facts about Danielle's current life. No toys, no school pictures. There were no children in this house. No sign of the big family Dani had always wanted to have. She'd always wanted to be a young mom, with two or three babies before she hit 30.

She's still got time to make that happen, Gemma thought.

Gemma wanted to ask her about it, but now was not the time. They'd just come back into one another's lives, and it was a heavy topic to broach.

What if the reason Danielle didn't have children was because Clay didn't want them? Then the conversation would quickly deteriorate, with Gemma unable to disguise her dislike and distrust of the man Dani had chosen to marry. Dani had chosen Clay over her. Period. There was no point pouring toxic waste all over the time they were spending together now, no matter how small of a window of time that would be, no matter the reason behind the reunion.

"Of course, the kitchen is back that way," Danielle said, pointing to where they'd just left. "And the bedrooms are this way."

Gemma trailed Dani down the hallway, where she opened the closed doors one by one.

The bedrooms told Gemma more of the story.

"This is mine and Clay's," Dani said. "Excuse the mess."

There was no mess.

The room was tidy enough to have been a rarely used guest room, everything from the rug to the throw pillows in pastel shades of green.

Very tranquil, Gemma thought. There's that word again. *Like a spa.*

The two other bedrooms left an unsettled feeling in Gemma's bones.

Each had a twin-size bed, a nightstand, and a small dresser. One of the other had walls the shade of pink everyone associated with baby girls. The other was painted a light blue. But, otherwise, neither was decorated yet.

These rooms had been intended for children.

"Pick either one," Dani said, uncertainly. "Or…"

She let her voice trail off, a third option unsaid hanging in the air.

"So, no kiddos yet?" Gemma asked as they walked to the last door at the end of the hallway. She'd wanted to wait, but with all the evidence piling up, it felt more insensitive *not* to say anything at this point. But she put every ounce of strength she could muster into keeping her tone light, hopeful.

"No," Danielle said in almost a whisper. "It's not the right time yet. Clay and I both want them, though. Soon, hopefully."

Gemma let out a relieved breath.

"Yes, soon," Gemma replied, trying to sound optimistic, hopeful, even. "The Jaegers can't end with us!"

"Clay and I want at least four children," Dani said, her voice growing watery. "But now… Maybe we shouldn't have put it off."

"He's going to be alright, Dani," Gemma assured her, even though her statement had no basis in fact or even probability. Dani had said he was fighting for his life, but Gemma hadn't asked for the details of Clay's condition. "What are the doctors saying?"

"They're…" Dani hesitated, sounding weepy. "Baffled. By his injuries. And you don't know he's going to be alright."

"You're right. I don't. But I sincerely hope he will be."

Dani didn't say anything as she made her way down the hall.

"You know," Danielle paused, her hand hesitant on the doorknob of the last closed room. "I prepared this room for you right after we moved in. I never intended for us to… I always hoped you would come at some point. Not because of a circumstance like this, obviously."

Gemma froze, shocked. She didn't know what to make of this revelation. Danielle wanted Gemma to come? Had hoped she would? All this time?

Had she been waiting for Gemma to make the first move?

She always did, you idiot. You're the big sister!

Gemma had always needed to make the first move, but with the way Danielle left, it had felt different. Dani had wanted space. Distance. She'd made that clear. Gemma had only let Dani go because that's what Dani had wanted. What Dani and Clay had wanted.

But now, standing in this hallway, peeking into the room that had clearly been intended for her, Gemma wondered what Dani had actually wanted. Had Gemma been too stubborn to see anything beyond her own feelings of abandonment? Had she been the one keeping them apart?

"Oh, Dani. I had no idea." Gemma's eyes welled up with tears, realizing their relationship could have been mended long ago.

But there was no going back, and truth be told, they shared responsibility for the time lost.

"Yeah. But it was never the right time," Dani added, and Gemma's heart deflated a bit.

Beams of sunshine filtered through the sheer white curtains, bouncing off the light sand-colored walls, and casting rectangular shadows on the full-size bed in one corner of the room. On the walls hung paintings of cities they'd been to when traveling with their parents, though Gemma was skeptical that Danielle had ever told Clay about that. Mountaintops, deserts, beaches, and forests.

Each one a significant moment in their training as hunters.

As a bonus, there was also a matching desk and dresser matching in light, birch wood. The room felt like the end of summertime, right before it turns cold, when everything glows with golden hues.

The desk was wide enough for Gemma to spread out multiple books while studying. That would come in handy for this particular visit.

"The room is perfect," Gemma said, blinking. She wiped at damp cheeks.

She didn't turn around to face her sister, scared the few tears she'd shed would turn into a full-on ugly cry if she looked Dani in the eyes. Pulling her laptop from her backpack, she placed it on the desk, while the backpack ended on the floor with her bag.

Danielle hung back at the doorway, leaning against the frame. "I'm glad you like it."

Gemma glanced over her shoulder as Dani fiddled with a fleck of loose paint, seeming to need the distraction. "I just hope the bed is comfortable enough for you. I know how you like a hard bed."

"I'm glad you remember that," Gemma said with a forced laugh. "I thought I might have to sleep on the floor."

She'd hoped the joke would lighten things up. It felt as if they were in a delicate bubble that could burst at any moment. Something inside Gemma pulsed with both the weight of unsaid words and the unfamiliar feeling of being *home*. Because, at the end of the day, that's what Danielle was. Home. She was the only person who knew Gemma inside and out. They'd grown up together. Experienced so many of the same things. Shared so many secrets.

She'd always known how much she missed Dani, but

she'd never let herself feel it until now. And she felt it, full force.

They walked back towards the kitchen, and Gemma was hit with a familiar smell that made her mouth water and stomach grumble. How had she been so intent on hating the place when they first came through the kitchen, her nose had refused to even acknowledge the delicious scent?

"Is that..."

The aromatic blend of onion and garlic, ginger and soy sauce, wok-fried meat and steaming rice was unmistakable.

Dani nodded. "I thought you might be a little hungry when you got in."

"You remembered," she said, touched at a gesture that meant so much more than getting her empty belly fed.

"How could I forget?" Danielle asked, softly.

After a long hunt, their parents would always reward the girls with Chinese takeout. It was a ritual Gemma had always indulged in with nothing less than rapture. The fact that it brought up warm, happy memories was just a bonus. She'd been unable to stomach her favorite meal for the past five years, but now, she couldn't wait to dig in.

Dani waved toward the kitchen counter, where three brown paper bags waited. "Fried rice and shrimp egg rolls. Sweet and sour chicken. Steamed pork buns. The whole shebang."

"Thank you," Gemma said simply.

Danielle busied herself with pulling out the containers and opening the food, but she paused to smile over her shoulder at Gemma. It was a sad smile, but a genuine one.

"No, sis," Dani said. "Thank *you*."

The conversation screeched to a sudden halt as Gemma watched her sister. For a moment, underneath the worry and exhaustion and fear, she caught a glimpse of Dani's youthful, carefree spirit. The way Dani was before the terrible night that robbed them of their parents and, ultimately, each other.

She'd never forgotten how much she loved her sister, but like she'd let the booze obliterate reality, she'd let her bitterness make that love seem like a hazy, faraway thing, instead of what it was. Eternal. Indestructible.

Gemma would go to the ends of the earth to protect Dani.

She stood there for a long moment, wondering what to do next, what to say next, but paralyzed by the weight of needing to get it right. What if, despite the strength of her love, they couldn't repair what was damaged?

It'll never be the way it was again. It can't. We're both different people now.

Before Gemma could untangle herself from the knots of indecision, Danielle turned quickly. She grabbed the car keys from where they hung beside the back door.

"Oh," Gemma tried not to let her disappointment show in her voice. "You're not going to have anything?"

"I need to get back to Clay. But help yourself to as much food as you like, and I'll be back as soon as I can, okay?"

Gemma took a deep breath and steadied herself. Even if they both wanted to reconcile, burned bridges didn't get rebuilt overnight.

Of course, Dani wouldn't want to share a meal, to catch up, right now. Clay was her top priority. Until they had kids, he would continue to be. Gemma needed to accept that fact and stop resenting it.

"I do need to ask you a few questions before you go," Gemma said.

Dani glanced at the door, clearly torn.

"If I'm going to find out what happened to Clay, there are things I need to know. And you know that," Gemma added.

Dani sighed, but gamely said, "Okay. Shoot."

"For starters… Ms. Coffey said Clay was attacked by a wild cat? Where did they get that idea? Do you think Clay said something?"

Dani squeezed her eyes closed and tears rolled down her cheeks. When she looked at Gemma again, she said, "He hasn't regained consciousness since the attack, so no."

"Oh. I'm so sorry, Dani. I didn't realize—"

"Well, you didn't ask, but… Anyway, it's not like *I* could tell anyone it was a Fury," Dani shrugged. "And since no one had ever seen any wounds like a Fury's talons would have left on Clay, they assumed it was the work of something with claws. A wild cat being the most obvious choice. This isn't bear country."

Gemma considered this. "Did you see the wounds yourself?"

Dani shook her head.

"They wouldn't let me."

Gemma's brows raised. Since when did the Jaeger girls let what they did and didn't do be dictated by what people would let them do?

Dani's eyes filled with tears. "I tried. I swear. But Ms. Coffey insisted I not look."

"Ms. Coffey was there?"

Dani nodded. Then she must've caught the look of suspicion Gemma felt flit across her face. "She's a little old lady, Gemma. I overheard one of the paramedics say the skin on Clay's chest and abdomen was shredded into ribbons. Ms. Coffey did not do that."

"Alright," Gemma allowed. "And that sounds… like Clay was brutally maimed. I agree. But," she paused. She didn't want to make Danielle angry or make her feel like Gemma was invaliding her thoughts. But facts were facts. "I still don't see any hard evidence that what happened to Clay was the work of a Fury."

"I *heard* it," Dani said, the claim certain and firm. "There's your evidence."

This made Gemma pause.

"… But you said you were sleeping. That the sirens from the ambulance woke you up."

"I was. They did. But I *remember* hearing it. It must've filtered in through my subconscious."

Gemma pressed her lips together. She studied her sister's face. Dani was not going to waver on this point. "Are you *sure*, Dani?"

"Are you doubting that I know what a Fury sounds like, Gemma?" Dani snapped, her voice cracking on Gemma's name.

"Of course I don't doubt that."

Their parents, Rayden and Taylor Jaeger, made certain both of their daughters were experts in the field of preternatural creatures: their habits, their vulnerabilities, their strengths and weaknesses, and of course, how to kill them. But before you could kill what you were hunting, you had to be able to identify it, even if the only clue you had to go by was the sounds it made.

"I heard it," Dani repeated, adamant. Hand on her hip. Foot tapping against the tile.

"Okay but maybe, you were having a nightmare? Is it possible it *was* a wild cat and you heard that and—"

"Can you please at least investigate before you dismiss what I'm telling you as impossible?" Dani asked.

"Of course, I will. That's why I'm here. But… how bad is it, Dani?" Gemma quickly asked, her voice laced with concern. "What have they told you about his odds?"

"He came through surgery fine—it took hours because there were some serious internal injuries—but he's in a medically induced coma. The pain would be too much to endure, even with the strongest of meds, they said. It also looks like he took a pretty bad blow to the back of his head. He probably hit the ground hard when, you know…"

So. No chance of Clay just opening his eyes and saying, "a Fury did it!" or "a mountain lion did it!" and putting the whole mystery to rest.

"Where did the attack happen? I didn't see any crime scene tape?" Though that didn't surprise her. Crime scene tape was not exactly fitting with Harmony Springs' aesthetic.

"That's because it's not being treated as a crime. But it happened in the side yard," Dani pointed in that direction with a shudder.

"Alright. I'm going to take a good look around the property while you are gone. Check and see if anything got missed by Barney Fife."

Dani rolled her eyes. "We're not Mayberry, Gemmie."

"Really? Because I'm pretty sure I saw Opie ride by on his bike on my way in."

That got a small smile out of Dani.

Their father had loved The Andy Griffith Show. At one point in time, both Jaeger sisters had known many episodes by heart, able to act out whole scenes from memory.

"You have my number if you need anything," Dani said. "But try to eat before you do anything else. I haven't forgotten how you are when you're on a mission."

What Dani meant was that Gemma tended to forget anything but the mission, including necessities, like food and water. She'd gotten dehydrated on a hunt more than once.

"Be careful out there," Gemma called, as Dani headed out.

"You be more careful!" Dani called back.

Piling as much rice as she could on the plate, Gemma placed it in the microwave to reheat. While she waited for the ding, she looked in the refrigerator for something to drink. Her heart fell as she took in the rows of beer bottles. Staying sober in this situation was already hard enough. A quick sip of something to take the edge off her nerves would have been more than welcome, but she hadn't come this far to screw it all up now. Gemma pushed the beers aside, hoping to find some juice or soda. If not, she'd settle for tap water.

But she found the pitcher of lemonade in the back, and she poured herself a tall glass just as the microwave went off.

She tried to eat the food slowly, cherishing every bite. But it was too good. The flavors exploded like fireworks on her tongue. She found herself shoveling the next bite in before she could even finish chewing the last until her stomach groaned at her, letting her know she'd reached her limit. She washed it down with the lemonade.

And then, it was time to do a bit of looking around.

She had no idea what she might find, but she was certain there would be no evidence of a Fury.

ONCE GEMMA FINISHED HER MEAL, SHE WALKED THROUGH the house again, this time at her own pace, not Dani's. With a critical eye. Even though she'd never been here before, if anything was amiss, she'd spot it. Her footsteps echoed softly against the hardwood floors. The front of the house had large arched windows with no blinds or curtains for privacy. She could see out, which meant *anyone* could see in.

There was a vase of flowers on almost every surface, the soft curves of their petals a striking contrast against the gleaming wood and hard edges of the coffee and end tables they sat upon. The overstuffed sofa and matching recliners all looked like places a person could curl up with a book and a throw blanket and nap peacefully for hours. There was no television.

Hmm.

Dani had always been a bit of a TV fanatic, so that was strange.

Glancing at the pictures on the walls, resentment rose inside Gemma. The only photos she recognized were the ones taken in East Haven, when Danielle married Clay. Clay, who was quite a bit older. Danielle, wearing a simple white gown, smiled at the camera. Clay looked down at her, his arms in a possessive hold around her middle as if to say, *Now you are mine.* There were no pictures of either of the couple as kids. There were no pictures of family or friends. Not even a picture of either of their parents. Not a single captured memory from before their wedding day. It was as if Danielle's life before Clay had been erased from this reality.

"Probably Clay's idea."

For Dani's sake, she hoped the man recovered and lived a long and healthy life. But Gemma had never liked him and never would.

Gemma closed her eyes, suddenly light-headed, as the past reached out and grabbed her, shaking her hard.

THE JAEGERS WERE AN UNUSUALLY tight-knit family, so it came as a surprise to no one when Gemma turned 18 and had no desire to venture out on her own. College had never really been in her plans. No university had a degree in Preternatural Hunting. A few years later when Dani hit the same milestone birthday, she made the same decision. So they were both in their 20s, living quite happily with their parents, in their childhood home. It was an unconventional arrangement, for sure, but well. Nothing about their family was conventional.

When two shots rang out that night, Gemma had at first thought she was dreaming.

Then she heard Dani's screams.

She hesitated, her bravery faltering.

Realistically, she probably only froze for seconds, but it felt like an eternity.

By the time she got herself out of bed and down the hall, it was too late.

She could have grabbed a weapon. She could have run to help. She could've intervened.

She could've saved her parents.

No one, not even Danielle, knew how responsible she felt for her parents' death, and they never would. Once she had to quit covering the pain of it with drinking, she'd done her best to avoid feeling all together. It was easier that way.

At least, it had been until she got the call from Danielle last night.

They'd both been wrecks after their parents were killed, but for Dani, it was different.

She hadn't only witnessed their death, she'd been attacked, too.

Left for dead, with no recollection of what had happened.

She quit speaking, eating, and taking care of herself, becoming nearly catatonic. Not knowing how to help her, Gemma arranged for her to go to a mental hospital. It killed her inside to feel like she was giving up on her sister. But Danielle would get care that Gemma herself didn't know how to give from the medical professionals at the highly rated Peaceful Pines.

With their parents gone and Danielle in an unresponsive state, Gemma had been a woman on a mission: Finding the monster that destroyed her family. Turns out, it was a mere mortal. That was the hardest lesson of all to wrap her mind around. She'd never imagined that the humans the Jaegers helped protect could be just as deadly and inhumane as the preternatural creatures they protected them from. Worse, though there'd been enough evidence at the scene to prove the suspect was human, there had not been enough evidence to catch anyone, much less convict.

In her ceaseless search, Gemma had been in constant contact with Clay Hickman, the detective in charge of the case. Even though Gemma had been raised to not trust the police, she had no one on her side but Clay. He'd been the first person at the crime scene and the last person to give up. She'd considered him a partner, in a way. But though they both worked tirelessly to track down the person responsible, there were no leads, no evidence. He didn't want to stop investigating—or so he claimed—but his superiors declared the case cold and demanded he transfer it and move on.

"I feel terrible," Clay had explained when he called her to let her know he was off the case. "But there's nothing I can do. My hands are tied."

That was fine. Gemma's hands weren't tied. She continued in her relentless pursuit.

And Clay?

Once he heard about Danielle's hospitalization, he began visiting her. It was sweet at first. He'd show up on a weekend afternoon here and there to sit with her or read her a book. But then the visits increased in frequency, until he was showing up three to four times a week. Sometimes more. Gemma started to get suspicious of his motives.

At first, she believed that maybe he had some lead he hadn't let her in on, that he was still working the case without her, trying to get some kind of info that existed only in the locked-down vault of her sister's mind. Why else would he be keeping such close tabs on Dani, seeing her so often?

Gemma insisted the nurses keep an eye on him and report every interaction between him and Danielle to her.

Danielle never said a word to Clay or anyone else. But according to the reports Gemma got from the nurses, Clay would talk to Danielle about anything and everything.

Then, one fateful day, the staff called Gemma in a rush to inform her that Danielle had spoken.

"Clay told Danielle he was afraid of rollercoasters, and she said *so am I*! She said *so am I*!" the nurse marveled.

It had been six months, but Danielle had finally spoken.

Gemma should have been happy. She knew she should. But she couldn't fight the jealousy that Clay had been the one to finally break through Danielle's impenetrable fortress of silence when she hadn't even come close. It stung in a way she couldn't fully describe. But she pushed away her feelings of betrayal, because she didn't want to make the wonderful miracle of her sister's breakthrough about her own pain.

She should have been elated when Danielle got better and came home. But instead, she felt like a failure.

Whoever killed their parents, whoever sent Dani spiraling into a prison of her own mind was still out there.

And Gemma grew increasingly uneasy when Clay was present.

Something was off about him. Nothing she could put to words, just a silent whisper in her gut. *Do not trust that man.* Every time he came around, she was overwhelmed with bad feelings she couldn't shake, bad feelings she could barely conceal.

She was completely floored when Danielle one day— giddily!—announced she and Clay were dating. In fact, by the time Danielle revealed the relationship to Gemma, she was already *in love*. She said he was her best friend.

But you've always said I *was your best friend,* Gemma thought, feeling childish.

She and Danielle had always been there for each other. They needed each other more than ever now. Or rather, Gemma needed Danielle more than ever. But now Dani had Clay. After so long of it just being the Jaeger girls against the world, Clay was what Danielle needed to pull her through now.

"He knows my pain, Gemma," Danielle told her more than once.

What the hell did that even mean?

Gemma was her sister! They'd lost both of their parents in one fell swoop.

How could anyone understand Dani's pain better than Gemma did?

Dani's declaration hurt Gemma more than Danielle could ever know.

She felt useless and discarded.

She'd just gotten Dani back and now she was losing her again?

And when Dani and Clay married dizzyingly soon after?

That burned through her entire soul.

It wasn't petty jealousy. It was the hopeless abandonment of the only person who knew you were drowning seeing you going under and turning away instead of diving in after you.

Danielle had always leaned on her. And that was fine. Gemma was the big sister. That was her job. But the one time Gemma needed to lean on Danielle, Danielle announced she was moving to Harmony Springs with Clay.

"Clay and I are moving to the house Mom and Dad left me in Harmony Springs," Dani said over lunch, one day, as casually as if she was commenting on the weather.

"What?" Gemma demanded.

Dani nodded. "I mentioned the house to him one day and he's been trying to convince me it was the right move ever since. Everything he said makes sense."

Gemma was stunned. Speechless.

"I want a normal life, Gemma. I want to leave East Haven and everything in it behind. It's what's best for me."

"What about me?"

"Right now, I need space from all the bad memories."

"So that's what I am? A bad memory?"

"Gemma..." Dani took a deep breath. "For now... for the time being... Clay and I believe that I need to sever all ties with the past."

Gemma had wanted to beg. To do whatever it took to change Dani's mind. But instead, the hurt part of her soul who couldn't bear any more rejection said, "Consider them severed."

———

GEMMA SNAPPED out of her painful reverie. With purpose, she went back to the bedroom to retrieve a weapon. Since she had no idea what she was dealing with, she got a handgun and a knife. Not her preference, but it's not like she could stroll through a neighborhood in Harmony Springs armed with a rifle or a crossbow.

Dani needed her again. Fuck the past. Gemma was going to be there for her now. Now. Not the past or the future. Her attention couldn't be divided. The present situation needed to be her sole focus. Even if that awful voice deep down still whispered, *You know she only needs you because Clay's out of commission. As soon as he's better, she'll be happy to send you back on your way to East Haven!*

She holstered the revolver underneath a jacket she wore for the sole purpose of concealing her weapon. She certainly didn't need it for warmth. Then she tucked the blade into her waistband careful not to accidently nick her flesh or slice her favorite pair of jeans.

She made her way outside, marveling again at the perfect weather.

Immediately, a bone-biting chill ran through her body, despite the fact that it wasn't cold or even cool out.

She felt exposed.

Someone is watching me, she thought.

She shook her head.

It was probably just Miss Coffey or another Harmony Springs busybody.

Focus!

Walking off the back patio, Gemma hoped she could quickly and easily find some missed clues that proved Clay's attacker had been human. Then she could leave the investigation to the police—though she doubted Harmony Springs PD was competent. But regardless, she could then focus on being there for Danielle in a purely sisterly capacity.

And Dani could drop the Fury theory.

Dani and I have both left that life behind, Gemma thought. *Please don't let it be a Fury.*

The hairs on the back of her neck stood on end. Despite what her eyes were telling her, her body seemed to be screaming that someone was near her. Watching. Waiting.

She swallowed hard and smoothed her hands over her ponytail and continued on.

You're just being paranoid, she told herself, even though that wasn't really something she did. Her gut was usually spot on.

After an hour of battling with her flight or fight response, there was still nothing of substance to report. The only footprints she could find were probably from the so-called wildlife officers. She couldn't find a trace of blood.

There was no evidence of any kind of attack. Period.

"What the hell," Gemma growled under her breath.

She had gotten nowhere.

Maybe it *had* been a mountain lion.

Hopefully Clay would wake up soon and he could tell them what happened.

She caught a movement out of the corner of her eye, from near the neighbor's house across the street. Miss Coffey's house.

Her hand steadied itself on her revolver, almost on its

own volition, her training deeply instilled in her like muscle memory.

She rounded the corner of the house and focused in on the location of the movement when she caught it again. It was subtle, clearly intended to not be noticed, but whoever it was had greatly underestimated her observation skills. The curtain of one of the windows in the house rippled in the soft breeze. The window was open.

Why would she leave her window open with a dangerous wildcat on the loose?

Gemma dropped her hand from the gun and extracted her phone from her back pocket. She quickly snapped a couple of pictures. One of Miss Coffey's opened window. Then she turned around to capture the perspective of what Miss Coffey would see from said window.

How much time did Miss Coffey spend looking out of that window, watching, and waiting for something to happen?

Gemma would guess a lot.

Had she seen Clay's attack? Did she witness something she was too afraid to tell the truth about? Did she maybe think the police wouldn't believe her report?

Gemma needed to find out.

She idly ran her hand up the side of the house as she continued to survey her surroundings. To the left. To the right. Up. Down.

Then she saw it.

She knelt, and there in the soft dirt beside the house were animal tracks. Small. Racoons. She was certain of it. They had probably been in the garbage. It was a high possibility that was why Clay came outside.

She could picture it all in her mind. Clay had heard a scuffling coming from outside. Acting as Dani's knight in shining armor, he'd gone outside to confront the source of the sound.

Maybe he had been surprised and hadn't only found raccoons, but a larger animal drawn out from the woods by the promise of a raccoon-shaped dinner.

There was nothing preternatural here, Dani, she would comfort her sister, once she was sure. *Our brains go there on instinct and probably always will. It's where they were trained to go. But it was likely a mountain lion in this case.*

But what if Dani was right?

The thought crept up her spine like a spider.

Looking up towards the sky, as if she was talking to her mother and father, Gemma simply said, "I've been out of this way too long. I have no idea what I'm doing. But I can't screw it up. I just can't."

Common sense told her not to go into the woods alone, but it didn't stop her from debating it. There had to be answers somewhere, even if they were deep in the underbrush.

She turned back to the house, debating going back inside to change into clothes more suited for a hike in the forest. It was then that she noticed something she'd missed because she'd been looking outward from the house, not toward it. But an enormous and obvious set of gouges had been made high up in the siding by an animal's claws. She stopped dead in her tracks, her breath catching in her throat.

The claws had first dug in, deep and jagged, at least five or feet above Gemma's head. They ended just below her eyeline as razor-thin scratches. Whatever it was had been up there, in the air, striking downward.

So not a wildcat, then.

Still holding her phone, she zoomed in and took a picture.

Her heart sank as she examined the screen. Just as Dani had been sure what she'd heard. Gemma was sure of what she was seeing.

They say a picture is worth a thousand words, and in this case, all of those words were swear words.

Because this picture confirmed Gemma's worst fears.

Gemma and her sister had grown up hunting the preternatural. Then they'd both given up that life. But it didn't matter.

They were back in it now, like it or not, and on the other side of the hunt.

Dani was right.

A Fury had been here. And since it hadn't finished the job, it would likely be back.

CHAPTER 6

Back inside the house, Gemma settled into her borrowed room. She fired up her laptop, determined to learn as much as she could about Harmony Springs and Clay's activities there. She hadn't asked Dani for the Wi-Fi password, so she'd have to use her phone as a hotspot for now.

Though Gemma didn't know *why* Clay had been attacked by a Fury, at least she knew what she was up against now.

Furies weren't creatures you generally had to worry about. You stayed away from them, they stayed away from you. On the other hand, if you pissed one off…

"What did you do, Clay?" Gemma muttered.

She knew Dani would be adamant her dear husband had done no wrong, but facts were on Gemma's side.

Furies had to be provoked.

Period.

But no amount of demanding answers from Clay would get her anywhere, since the man was in a medically induced coma. So Gemma's first step was figuring out what a Fury might be doing in Harmony Springs.

Had Clay been out of town, and done something there to lure the Fury here?

Gemma scrawled on her notebook: *Has Clay traveled anywhere lately?*

Then she went back to her web research.

There were no news articles to be found other than fluffy, filler pieces about knitting club at the library and things like that. No mentions of robberies, police activity, or even bad weather. It was as if nothing negative had ever happened in Harmony Springs. Just as Matt had told her, there seemed to be no *real* news about Harmony Springs.

Judging from everything she found on the internet, despite what Danielle said, this entire town was so Mayberry it might as well actually be in black and white. All signs pointed to this being a tranquil, quiet town where everyone coexisted in… harmony.

But that couldn't be right.

Gemma knew people. And where people were, there was drama. There was crime, there were accidents. There was no way a town existed, especially a town where everyone knew everyone, where everything was perfect and always had been. She should at least be able to find one instance of something having gone awry in this godforsaken town.

She'd heard of cities' governments wiping their entire online history clean after a preternatural attack, to cover it up. Could that be what was happening here? Maybe. But it was more than that. Half of the world wide web seemed to be inaccessible. She couldn't even get a single search engine to pull up any results about Furies when she tried to look them up, nor did Clay seem to exist. There'd been plenty of articles written after the death of her parents, with Detective Clay Hickman quoted as a source. But none of those were even coming up.

"Ugh, this is so damn useless." She groaned in frustration and closed her laptop.

There has to be a way to find out more about this town's history.

The town's *real* history, not the stub of an article on Wikipedia that gushed about the town's founder and what a wonderful philanthropist she was, with no further information. Not even the woman's name or the year she'd founded Harmony Springs.

Gemma felt inept and ill-equipped. If she couldn't even handle the research side of things, how was she supposed to take down a Fury? Or even *find* it.

Mom would know what to do. Dad would know what to do.

She thought.

Randy.

He might be able to give her some perspective. She found his name in her contacts and called without hesitation, so grateful he'd come back into her life when he did.

He picked up on the first ring.

"What's up, girl? Didn't expect to hear from you." She could hear the smile in his deep, raspy voice. Her hunched shoulders relaxed at the sound.

She quickly gave him the rundown of the past 24 hours. How Danielle called her the evening before, how Clay had been the victim of a Fury attack, how she seemed to be at an impasse.

"I can't find anything of substance about Harmony Springs online. For all intents and purposes, they make it look like this place is all bake sales and porch swings. But nowhere is this squeaky clean, Randy."

"Well, that right there tells you they may have something to hide now, doesn't it?"

"And it's not just that. The problem is it's like Harmony Springs is limiting the information people here get about, well, everything. Even my bar's website shows it is in maintenance mode. Now, I'm not positive it isn't, but…"

Randy didn't reply but faint clicks of a keyboard came from his end of the line. "It isn't," he confirmed. "I'll look into all this right now."

Though no one would ever guess it from his appearance, Randy was quite the computer whiz. He preferred that phrasing to the term hacker. He was truly one of those books you couldn't judge by a cover.

"Is there anything else I can help you with?"

Gemma didn't want to say it, but her gut feeling was rarely wrong. She had to trust it.

"Yeah, can you check into Clay's background also?"

"Your brother-in-law?"

"Clay Hickman. But he goes by Clay Smith now."

"I assume you don't know the reason behind the name change?"

"You assume right." Blowing out her breath in a rushed sigh, she replied, "There's no way you can access his phone records, right? I'd like to know where he's been recently, if he's left town."

Randy let out a long whistle. "I know a guy. Consider it done, Gem."

With Randy now working on a computer with internet that functioned as it should, Gemma decided to call Harmony Springs Fish and Wildlife Service, but, of course, it was already closed for the day. A recorded message told her that they were only open from 10:00AM until 2PM every day.

"Small towns. Gotta' love them," Gemma said to no one as she made a note to make a visit there in the morning.

Gemma realized there wasn't much more she could do

for the day, short of wandering around calling, "Here Fury, Fury," and hoping the thing showed itself.

She was about to call Matt—the best way to ease her mind until Dani returned—when she thought she heard the front door creak open. Clutching her knife, blade out, Gemma crept to the front of the house.

"Oh my god, Gemma!" Danielle screamed as she rounded the corner. "You scared the hell out of me!"

"Sorry," Gemma said quickly as she slid the knife back into her waistband. "I wasn't expecting you home this soon."

She'd honestly started wondering if Danielle would spend the night at the hospital with Clay.

"I can see that," Danielle responded sarcastically, one hand still over her heart as she tried to catch her breath. "But it's getting late. I wanted to see you before you went to bed."

Gemma realized that it was dark outside.

Time flies when you're not having fun, too.

"I'll probably go back and spend the night there, though, if that's okay with you," Dani said.

"Any changes with Clay?"

Dani shook her head. "I wouldn't have left at all, but the nurse insisted I should come home, shower, and get some rest. She said she'd call me if he showed any signs of regaining consciousness. Even a twitching pinky, but… I want to be there."

Wait. Did people just spontaneously regain consciousness when under a medically induced coma?

Sliding her hand over her forehead, Danielle took a deep breath before releasing it slowly. "Until we get to the bottom of this, Clay may never be safe. Or me, for that matter. Furies never leave business unfinished. You know that."

And Furies never attacked unless for revenge or self-preservation, Gemma thought. *You know that.*

But there was no point in arguing with Danielle on this. Gemma was pretty sure her sister would insist Clay's shit didn't stink. No way would she ever be able to fathom that he'd brought the attack on himself some way.

"Is there anything you need?" Gemma asked, knowing that there was little she could do for her sister emotionally, but maybe there was some other way she could help.

"Food. I am starving," Danielle said, walking into the kitchen. "And I need to know what you've found out so far. If anything."

"I left quite a bit of the takeout," Gemma said.

"Did you want any more to eat?" Danielle asked as she opened the containers.

"Since you've twisted my arm, I'll have an eggroll. Maybe a wing. Just to keep you company."

"Mm-hmm," Danielle said, knowing better.

Gemma was incapable of resisting Chinese food.

The sisters shared a brief laugh, then the room was quiet except for the sound of their plastic forks scraping against paper plates. Though they could both wield a sword with precision, neither had ever mastered chopsticks.

Gemma could feel the tension in the air.

Make the first move.

But Dani spoke first. "Have you found out anything?"

"Let's eat first, give you a moment to breathe before we get into that," Gemma said changing the subject. She still wasn't sure how to navigate the reality of what had happened without stepping on an emotional land mine and blowing them both up. "How have you been, Dani?"

Gemma's sister looked at her for a long moment before responding. "How have I been?" she responded around a mouthful of food. She chewed and raised an eyebrow. "I've been great. Except for this attack, that is."

"Yeah, except for that," Gemma said softly. She filled her own mouth with a forkful of fried rice.

Everything fell silent again for a moment until Danielle put her fork down and focused her attention on Gemma. "I know you'll hate to hear this, Gems, but moving to Harmony Springs was the best thing for me."

What about me and what I needed?

God, would the anger never go away?

"But are you *happy*?" Gemma asked.

Maybe if Danielle was really and truly happy, maybe then Gemma could let it go and just be grateful for that.

"Happy," Dani repeated, running a hand through her hair, and seeming to contemplate the meaning of the word. "Well, I guess I'm happy I'm not hunting anymore. I don't miss it. And I am so fucking pissed this damn Fury brought *that* world into *this* life."

Gemma's hand stilled with an egg roll halfway to her mouth. The red sweet and sour sauce dropped onto the table, but she was too shocked to move.

Her mouth opened and closed a few times before she found the words.

"Really? You're *happy* you're not hunting anymore?"

"I know it goes against everything we were raised to believe, but I just couldn't do it anymore. Not after… not without…" Danielle's sentence trailed off as she gauged Gemma's reaction. Then she carefully continued, "I was only doing it because it's what was expected of us."

"Dani, I never knew that," Gemma whispered.

"You weren't supposed to," Dani whispered, looking directly into Gemma's eyes. Dani was stripped bare of all facades. The shame and fear of her sister's rejection evident in every muscle of her face. "*You* always did it because you loved it. I didn't think you'd understand. You were a natural. The best. I was never as good as you. You were born to be a Huntress."

Gemma shook her head. "The truth of the matter is, I quit hunting, too…"

Danielle stared at Gemma in disbelief. "*You?* I can't believe that."

"What I loved was working with you and our parents. Being a team. I think we could have been plumbers and I would've wanted it to never end. When all of you left me, I stopped hunting. And started drinking. I told myself I could drink like a fish and not drown, but I was wrong. I'm sober now, but I only stopped after I very nearly drank myself to death."

Gemma looked away; her eyes glassy with unshed tears. Now it was her turn to feel shame. When she looked back at her sister, Dani reached out and touched her arm.

"I'm so sorry you went through that, Gemmie. I'm sorry I wasn't there for you."

"If it wasn't for Matt…" Gemma trailed off, the tears in her eyes threatening to spill over.

"Whoa!" Danielle almost choked on her food. "Who is *Matt?* Are you *married?* You didn't mention it, but you aren't wearing a ring, so I assumed you weren't—"

"No, I'm very single and intend to stay that way. Matt is Matt Silva."

"Matt Silva?" Dani echoed, incredulously. "From elementary school?"

Gemma could feel her cheeks warming as she nodded. She silently reminded herself she should call him before it got too late.

"Don't get the wrong idea," she said to Dani. "Matt and I are friends. He happened to be there at the right time to get me to the hospital and I will forever owe him for that."

Danielle raised her eyebrows. She leaned her head forward skeptically but didn't say anything more. Sure, Gemma wasn't exactly telling the full truth, but Danielle had to know her well enough to know she wasn't just going to open a vein right here at the dining room table and spill her feelings everywhere.

"From the cat that ate the canary look on your face, I'm guessing he grew up to be hot *and* he has it bad for you," Dani said.

"I mean, he's not ugly," Gemma admitted, appreciating Dani's attempt to lighten the mood. "Yeah, he's hot."

"Annnnnnnnnd he has it bad for you."

Gemma rolled her eyes.

"Aha! I knew it. So why aren't you hitting it?" Dani demanded.

"I didn't say I wasn't," Gemma shot back. "We are friends. But. There may be benefits involved."

Dani laughed, truly delighted, then somberness and shame overtook her expression again, as if she was a horrible person for experiencing even a moment of joy under the circumstances.

They resumed eating for a few minutes, before Danielle groaned and declared herself done.

"Yeah," Gemma said. "I'm stuffed, too."

"So… wanna rock, paper, scissor for the last eggroll?"

Gemma laughed. "Loser has to eat it?"

"Please," Dani said. "Winner gets it."

"Or we could just split it."

"Deal."

Dani sawed it in two with a plastic knife and passed half to Gemma.

"Well, even if you won't admit that you've got a man, I

will say I'm so glad I have one who loves me and has been taking care of me. And I hope that if Matt Silva wants to love you and take care of you, you'll let him." She paused, absentmindedly pushing a single grain of rice around with her fork. "I've been so worried about you. In East Haven. Alone. I mean, I know you can take care of yourself, but…"

"We never found who killed Mom and Dad," Gemma completed her thought when Dani couldn't go on.

Danielle rubbed the corner of her right eye.

Then she continued, her voice barely above a whisper, "It was one of the reasons I agreed to move here with Clay. As long as we lived in East Haven, I always felt as if I should be looking over my shoulder. I was always terrified. *Always* on the verge of a panic attack. Always afraid he'd come back."

Then why did you leave me there?

"I had no idea," Gemma said.

Is that why she turned to and fell for Clay? Because she thought he could protect her better than her sister could?

"But I was there, Dani. You could have told me," she whispered. "I would have kept you safe. I would have never let anyone hurt you."

But deep down, she knew that was a promise she couldn't make. Dani had lived the night their parents died because the murderer had been unsuccessful in his attempt to kill her… not because Gemma did anything to save her. Gemma hadn't even moved quickly enough to scare the killer away. She didn't know why he fled without making sure Dani was dead. And she'd been too grateful that Dani had survived to tempt fate by questioning that fact.

"Gemma, I love you. You are my big sister, but it is not your job to take care of me. It never was. I am a grown woman. A grown married woman."

You can need your sister AND your husband, Gemma thought to herself. *But we'll table this conversation for now.*

They'd spent enough time discussing their own inner demons for the evening and now they needed to focus on the immediate concern, which was a very real danger right in their backyard. Well, Dani and Clay's backyard, anyway.

All of a sudden, Dani sobbed.

"What if he doesn't make it, Gemma?" she asked, her face contorted with despair.

Gemma scooted her chair close to Danielle and took her hand. "I'm sorry you have to go through this, but you are so strong. And you're not alone. I'm here."

Dani sniffled, and as if the possibility that her husband might had only been a passing, silly thought, she declared, "Clay's a determined man. When he puts his mind to something, it gets done. He'll pull through. He has to." She shook her head as if to clear it. "So, did you find anything while I was at the hospital?"

Gemma's heart beat like a drum in her chest as she nervously twisted her hands together. "Well, I'm certain that it was a Fury that attacked Clay."

"So, I was right." There was no victory in her tone. No celebration. She hadn't wanted to be right. She'd wished it was truly a wild cat.

"Yes, you were right. Now it's imperative we find out *why* Clay was attacked," Gemma said slowly.

"You think he's to blame, don't you?" Dani asked. She clenched her jaw. "You think he's guilty of something."

The fact Gemma had been trying to ignore had to be acknowledged and voiced out loud now.

"It was a female Fury, Dani," Gemma said, gently.

She pulled out her phone and showed Dani the irrefutable proof. The picture she'd taken of the gouges on the side of the house. Claw marks left by a male Fury looked completely different than those of a female Fury.

"So you think there was another woman," Dani said, as if that theory was completely out of left field.

"You know Furies don't attack out of some primal instinct," Gemma said.

"Yes."

"They only attack those who have crossed them in some way," Gemma said.

"Usually, but—"

"Always, Danielle," Gemma cut her off. "Always."

She didn't say the rest.

Nine times out of ten, female Furies were gorgeous when they were in human form. They were enchanting seductresses. And when they shifted and attacked... it was more often than not because they'd been scorned by a lover.

Dani stood. She slammed her palm down on the table. "I can't believe you think my husband could have been cheating on me. There is no way! None!"

Gemma wished she had the faith her sister had in Clay, but she just didn't. And even if she did, logic and experience taught her that Fury attacks didn't happen to innocent people. They were goddesses of vengeance, not psychopathic killers. If this were anyone else they were talking about, Dani would realize that, as well.

"I didn't say Clay was having an affair." *I thought it, but I didn't say it.* "What I said was there is evidence of a female Fury. That's it. We both know Furies attack those who have done them wrong. It's personal. It's always personal."

"Here we go again." Danielle threw her hands up and walked away.

"Believe it or not, I am trying to protect you, Dani," Gemma said as she followed her sister into the hallway.

"I know you are," Dani replied. But her tone was cold. She turned to face Gemma and warmth seeped back into her voice, "I do know you're trying to help, Gemma. But I can't believe that Clay would cheat on me. I won't. He just *wouldn't*. I know it in my bones. But regardless of why the Fury attacked him, we both know if she is unsuccessful on her first attack, she'll keep coming back."

Gemma sighed, wearied by the task at hand. The Fury could be *any* female. Because they transformed from human to Fury and back, discovering a Fury's true identity would be next to impossible.

At least Clay would be safe while he was in the hospital, surrounded by doctors and nurses and other patients. The Fury wouldn't risk harming innocents on her quest for vengeance. It just wasn't how they rolled.

"And if what you say about it being a female Fury is true, then it's not Mr. Owens from next door. Which was my prime suspect. He was the first one on the scene."

"Is he married?" Gemma asked before she thought about it.

"Yes, and his wife is 77, in case you were asking because you're looking for the woman you think Clay's been fooling around with. Who doesn't exist."

"Dani—"

Dani shook her head. "We're just going to have to agree to disagree on the Fury's motive."

"Alright," Gemma said. She shook her head, trying to wrap her mind around everything.

Danielle walked back into the kitchen and put her empty plate in the sink, her face blank as she rinsed off the food residue.

"Harmony Springs *is* a small town," Dani said, as she stared out of the kitchen window.

"Yep," Gemma had said, not sure what track Dani's

train of thought was on. They'd already covered how small Harmony Springs was.

"I *know* most of these people. I have a hard time believing one of them is a Fury. And... like I said... they're all older."

With a sigh, Gemma hesitated, not knowing if she should tell Danielle about the issues she was having with the internet. Something was fishy in this town. Was it really the utopia it seemed to be?

"You know *most* of the people who live here. But how well? And what about the ones you don't know?"

Dani shrugged. "It's a quiet little community. Most people here are old enough to be our grandparents."

Gemma thought of Miss Coffey. That old bitty seemed like the type of woman who had an axe to grind.

What if Clay wasn't having an affair, but he'd done something else to wrong one of the grannies of Harmony Springs?

There was no point in pursuing this theory with Dani.

"There was no sign of an attack in your yard. Was it Fish and Wildlife who cleaned things up?"

"I don't know," Dani said.

"Well, I plan to stop by their office in the morning," Gemma changed the subject. "Maybe they know something we don't."

It was likely a dead end, but you had to explore all the possibilities. Even the ones you thought would be useless. Even the ones you didn't like.

Danielle's brow furrowed as she looked over at her. "I don't know. But, hey, I'd like you to come to the hospital with me," she said. "After Fish and Wildlife, that is."

She reached out and squeezed Gemma's hand. It softened Gemma's heart.

"Clay is your husband." Gemma attempted to smile.

Her mouth turned up at the corners, but the muscles around her eyes remained slack. No matter how she tried to push past her disdain and mistrust, it was buried deep in her. "Of course, I'll go with you if you want me to. I'm here to help you with whatever you need."

Gemma started to clear the rest of the table, but Danielle told her she would take care of it.

"I just need something to keep me busy. Keep my mind occupied."

Gemma understood completely. Danielle didn't need to explain any further. Telling Danielle goodnight, she headed to her room.

Closing the door behind her, Gemma sat on the edge of her bed. She picked up her phone to call Matt before she went to sleep.

Toying with it, she hesitated for a moment before pressing the call button. "I know it's late, Matt," Gemma began when he answered, sounding sleepy. "I hope you weren't waiting for me to call."

"I wasn't. I was watching that zombie show you keep recommending."

"Oh," Gemma replied. "Okay."

He was such a terrible liar.

"How are you liking it? Don't you love Luke? He's my favorite character."

"Yeah, he's great."

Gemma burst out laughing, hoping Dani hadn't heard. She didn't want to seem insensitive.

"There is no Luke, is there?" Matt asked.

"Well, I'm sure there are indeed Lukes. Just not in that particular show," she said, falling back on the bed and letting her head hit the pillow.

"How's your brother-in-law? Is Danielle holding up okay?" Matt asked.

"Do you actually mind if we don't talk about that?" Gemma asked.

It was nice to talk about something normal for a second with someone who thought the preternatural existed only in television shows and movies. She felt pretty certain as soon as she went to sleep, the nightmares would begin. And when she woke up? Well, tomorrow might be worse than any nightmare her imagination could conjure tonight.

CHAPTER 7

Gemma woke later than she usually did from a surprisingly dreamless and uninterrupted sleep.

It took her half a minute to realize where she was.

Listening to the sounds of the house, the slight movements of Danielle shuffling about told Gemma it was clearly time to get up. But she didn't really want to. The sheets were a higher thread count than her own, so soft against her skin. The mattress was just the right firmness. She wanted to lie there for a while, pretend she'd come to visit Danielle for the sole purpose of seeing her and spending time with her. That they were in no hurry. They had nothing to do.

But that wasn't the case.

She needed to talk to the warden of Fish and Wildlife as soon as she could. He or someone he supervised may've seen something that meant nothing to them… but might give Gemma a vital clue to the Fury's identity. Quickly showering and getting dressed, Gemma joined Danielle in the living room.

Danielle sat in one of the recliners, clutching a cup of coffee and flipping through a photo album. She didn't notice Gemma at first, so Gemma quietly observed her.

The effect the attack was having on Danielle was clear from the tense set of her shoulders all the way down to the slight tremble in her fingers.

"How long have you been up?" Gemma asked, finally.

When Danielle looked at her, the dark circles underneath her eyes made Gemma wonder if she'd slept at all.

"Not long," she started, but then shook her head. "I mostly laid awake all night, really. The bed smelled like us, like him… and him not being there… it made it worse. I ended up stripping off the bedding and putting on some fresh sheets. But then I felt like I was trying to erase him, so I put the old sheets back on. Finally fell asleep at about five in the morning but it didn't last long. I called the hospital like fifteen times, to make sure there had been no change. The nurses are going to hate me."

Glancing at the clock, Gemma noticed it was just after eight. "Has there been any change?"

Danielle shook her head.

"Well, I mean. No news is good news, right?"

Danielle shot her a skeptical look.

Their father had always said *no news* meant you weren't looking hard enough. He said it with a questioning lilt and raised eyebrows, as if it was merely something he wanted them to think about.

I wish you were here now, Dad, Gemma thought, with a pang.

Gemma changed tactics, "Looking at pictures of you and Clay?"

"Looking at pictures, yeah," Danielle said, her voice faint, as if she was fading away right before Gemma's eyes.

For the first time Gemma let herself think the unimaginable. Danielle very nearly hadn't come back from the last trauma she experienced. What if Clay didn't make it and that sent her over the edge again, this time for good?

Gemma couldn't save her last time… what if this time there was no bringing her back?

"Oh," Gemma said, her stomach suddenly in knots.

"They're pictures of you and me," Dani said.

"Really?" Gemma asked, surprised.

Moving further into the living room, she sat next to Danielle and looked in the box.

"Clay didn't want me to keep them, so I hid them. I didn't have the heart to leave them behind."

Gemma clenched her jaw, grinding her teeth to keep her judgmental thoughts inside.

What kind of marriage do you have if you must hide childhood pictures from your spouse? What kind of man wants his wife to throw out her childhood memories?

Gemma was surprised that Dani told her any of this, but she was glad her sister felt safe enough with her that she did.

Finally, she managed to say, fairly evenly, "I'm glad you kept them, Dani."

"So am I." Dani wiped tears away.

"Hey, look, this is from the Halloween mom tried to make our costumes," Gemma said, pulling out a picture. She chuckled, despite everything, still unsure of what their mother intended them *to be* that year. Their mom had been great with a sword, but terrible with a threaded needle.

"Oh my gosh! It is." Danielle's smile was the same now as it was in the picture. Except her two front teeth weren't missing anymore.

Gemma spotted a picture of herself holding Danielle shortly after she was born. The urge to keep her mouth tamed was overruled by her need to know.

"Why wouldn't he want you to have pictures of us growing up?" Gemma asked.

"Clay hoped it would 'keep the bad memories away,'

but these aren't bad memories." She looked at the photos with such sadness and longing that it made Gemma's heart ache.

"We were so innocent then. There were no monsters in our closet. Nothing bad in the world, that we knew of." Gemma's voice was quiet, barely above a whisper, but the pain was loud and clear. The same pain she felt every time she thought about those happy, carefree days.

"I know it sounds harsh, but he was trying to do what he thought was best for me. So please don't blame him." Danielle's words tumbled out in a rush.

Danielle's tone was pleading, and Gemma knew not to press the issue any further. She could see the pain in Danielle's eyes. It wasn't the time to push this line of questioning any further.

"So, Clay's not a cop anymore?" Gemma asked. She'd noticed a plaque on the wall from the Chamber of Commerce. It appeared her brother-in-law was an entrepreneur now, instead of a man of the law. Clay *Smith* owned Smith Consulting.

"Not much crime in Harmony Springs…" Danielle's voice trailed off. "When we arrived, there were no openings at the police department, so he started his firm instead."

"And… the two of you changed your last name from Hickman to Smith because…?" Gemma tried not to sound suspicious, but that part was just as weird to her as the presence of a Fury. If not more.

Dani shrugged. "For a fresh start."

Gemma wondered what the real reason was and if Dani even knew. What kind of fresh start required changing your surname? Unless you were joining the Witness Protection Program or something, which obviously wasn't the case.

"And whose idea was that?" Gemma asked and Danielle shot her a look that said *Really?*

"He snores. Are you going to find some deep meaning that signals he's an evil mastermind behind that, too?"

"Well, no, because you also snore," Gemma pointed out. "I need to know things, Dani. I wish you wouldn't take everything I ask as a personal offense."

"I wish you wouldn't ask everything as if you're trying to prove my husband guilty when he's the victim."

"I'm trying to find out what happened, Dani. Is that why you asked me to come here or not?"

Dani's shoulders slumped. "It is. It's just hard for me."

Gemma nodded. She got that.

"What kind of firm is Smith Consulting?" She couldn't imagine there was much business for *any* kind of firm in such a small town.

Dani lifted her chin. "Clay is well-liked, so he gets a lot of business through word-of-mouth."

Gemma bit her lip. Dani hadn't answered her question at all. Gemma made a mental note to find out what type of *firm* Clay had.

"I guess he must be doing well then," she commented.

"So well that I don't have to work, anyway. I have hobbies to keep me busy, and I'm involved with the Rotary Club." Danielle twisted her fingers nervously in her lap. Probably because she knew Gemma was wondering what the hell a Rotary Club was and why her young, vibrant sister would want to spend her time on one.

"What hobbies?" Gemma asked.

"Well, I crochet. Miss Coffey taught me how. I was learning to play the piano, but well. It was a struggle so Clay thought maybe I should try something else."

Of course and of course.

"I still love to swim, obviously, and there's a lot of

activities down at the community center, like yoga and Bunco nights."

So Dani was basically a retired senior citizen in a 20something body.

"Well. I should probably get to the Fish and Wildlife office," Gemma paused and looked at her sister. "You want to go with me?"

She wasn't surprised when Danielle shook her head.

"I've gotta get to the hospital. I really shouldn't have left him." The guilt was evident in her voice as if it was a physical weight pushing down on her.

"Dani, he's being taken care of," Gemma said softly.

"Not by me," Dani said.

Gemma heard her phone ringing from down the hall. Glad for the reprieve, she apologetically said, "Gotta get that."

"Might be Maaaaaaaaatt," Dani teased.

But it was Randy.

"Unfortunately, I don't have much for you," he said when Gemma answered. "My guy did a thorough search on his phone number, but didn't see any evidence of it pinging off any towers. Anywhere. So I can't tell you if he's been outside of Harmony Springs."

"That's super weird, right?"

"Yes. But what I can tell you is that Clay is self-employed at some kind of consulting firm in Harmony Springs. Looks like your basic nine-to-five. Like everything else in Harmony Springs, he seems squeaky clean."

Consulting what, though?

"Squeaky clean," Gemma harumphed. "Doubt that."

"Well, you never did like your brother-in-law," Randy laughed. "So, you might be a bit biased, kiddo."

Part of her hoped Randy was right, and *she'd* been wrong all this time. That Clay was really the stand-up

Prince Charming Danielle believed he was. But she couldn't ignore her intuition right now.

"Those feelings aside, I know what I'm doing, and I know when my gut is telling me something is off."

"Well, his finances seem a bit… unusual, so start there. I emailed you a compressed file of everything I managed to compile on Clay and Harmony Springs. Like I said, it's not much, but maybe you'll spot something I missed."

"Hopefully it'll come through," Gemma mused. "Thank you, Randy."

"Just be safe out there, okay, and tell your sister I asked about her."

"Will do," Gemma said, but she wasn't even sure she should mention she'd contacted Randy.

"You want to be honest with her, Gemma," Randy said, as if he could read her thoughts. "You might want to tell her everything. From what you've said, you two are on shaky ground right now. Lies and deception ain't gonna help matters."

Gemma rolled her eyes. "Lies and deception are Hunting 101, Randy. But I'll do my best. Thanks again for all the info."

Disconnecting the call, Gemma went to her laptop and searched for the email Randy sent her. It hadn't been blocked from coming through, which surprised her a bit. She decided to read Clay's file first.

He was attacked for some reason, and she had to find out what that reason was.

Looking at Clay's file, Gemma saw a pattern emerge. Randy wasn't kidding when he said Clay's financial situation was unusual. He was getting paid a large lump sum of money every three months and a few days later, exactly 75% of that was transferred out. There were no other deposits or withdrawals for operational expenses, no revenue stream to speak of.

She began making a few notations for Randy to check the next time she called him. She was certain he'd been thorough, but there had to be another bank account, another source of income. She didn't even see the evidence of a personal checking account, but if he didn't have one, where was he sending the transferred funds?

By her own admission, Danielle didn't work because she didn't have to.

I need to do some snooping, Gemma thought.

Luck was on her side for once. Dani had left a note in the kitchen saying she'd left for the hospital, and asking, again, for Gemma to meet her there after she'd gone to Fish and Wildlife.

But before I go to Fish and Wildlife…

There was one room Dani hadn't shown her in the quick tour of the Hickman/Smith home. Gemma half-expected that door to be locked, but it wasn't. A home office. With a laptop.

She sat down in front of the screen and stared at it for a moment before pushing the power button.

Of course, it was password protected.

She looked around for a Post-It note with the password on it, hopeful, but came up empty. She tried Dani's birthday, then their anniversary date. Both wrong. She closed her eyes, considering what to try next, since she didn't know Clay's birthday. ILoveDanielle? DanielleIsMine?

But when she looked back at the screen, her mouth dropped open at the warning message.

Reminder: After your fourth incorrect attempt, the hard drive will self-destruct.

"What?" she whispered.

Who the hell had those kind of fail-safe measures in place for a personal computer?

She powered the laptop down.

You are hiding something, Clay Hickman, she thought. *And for my sister's sake, I'm going to find out what it is if it kills me.*

———

THE PAVEMENT of Main Street was a smooth, black ribbon, unmarred by cracks or potholes.

Gemma located Clay's office and parked on the side of the building.

Inside, the lobby was lined with closed doors to the left and right. The walls were a light beige color with white crown molding at the top. The floor was a dark wood, and the furniture was modern and sleek.

This place looks like it belongs in a city, not in Harmony Springs, Gemma thought.

There were three receptionists.

Gemma strode toward the closest one.

Her hair was pulled back into a tight bun. She wore a crisp black suit with a white blouse underneath. Her nametag read Brynn.

The woman's eyes darted to the door and then the windows, before finally landing on Gemma with the plastic smile of a Barbie doll.

"How may I assist you today?" she asked.

"Hello, I'm Gemma, Clay Hic...Smith's sister-in-law."

Brynn's smile faltered. "Good morning, Miss Jaeger."

She stared at Gemma as if she was waiting on Gemma to do something for her.

I didn't tell you my last name, Gemma thought. *So how did you know it?*

She seriously doubted Clay had ever mentioned her

to this woman in casual conversation. What would he say? *Oh, yes, I have a sister-in-law named Gemma Jaeger who my wife and I abandoned back in their hometown. My wife never speaks to her because I completely isolated her from her former life. Ha ha ha!*

Shaking her head, Gemma cut right to the point.

"My sister sent me to pick up a few personal belongings Clay left in his office. She said you'd be able to let me in." Gemma's lie was spontaneous but smooth.

"You want to go in Mr. Smith's office?" Brynn stammered with wide-eyed dismay, as if Gemma had asked the woman to give her a bikini wax. Then she recovered with that same plastered on fake smile. "How rude of me. I didn't even ask. How is Mr. Smith doing?"

"As far as we know, he will pull through. My sister's at the hospital with him now and I'll be joining her in a little while. But I really do need to get into his office."

"Of course," Brynn said. "I can let you in."

"I would appreciate that."

Brynn came around the desk and started down the hall, her high heels clacking on the floor. Gemma followed. When they entered Clay's office, she was enveloped by the scent of leather and wood. A large, dark bookcase filled the entire right-hand wall. A leather couch sat nestled against the other wall with a fur rug on the floor between them. The far wall had a massive fireplace and mantle commanding the middle, with bookshelves lining it on both sides.

Gemma tried to open the drawer of the desk, but a slight pullback let her know it was locked tight.

"Do you have the key to his desk?" she asked Brynn.

"I don't."

Gemma could tell from Brynn's stiff movements and stilted speech that she wasn't going to get anywhere with this woman. Nor did it seem like Brynn was planning on giving Gemma any time alone in Clay's office.

Gemma pretended to look around. "Hmm." She furrowed her brow in an exaggerated manner, hoping to portray genuine confusion Brynn wouldn't overlook. "Dani —that's my sister, Mr. Smith's wife—said he left his favorite sweater here. But I don't see it anywhere. Maybe it's in his car. Anyway, thank you very much. I will let Clay know that you asked about him."

Gemma felt unsettled under Brynn's watchful eye, as if she were being studied.

"Oh," she said, suddenly, as if she'd forgotten. "Dani also wanted me to check and see if Clay had any upcoming appointments we'd need to cancel? Or do you take care of that?"

"Mr. Smith doesn't have any upcoming appointments."

"Really?" Gemma tried to keep her tone neutral. "You don't even... need to check?"

Brynn shook her head. "No. I don't."

Gemma's head cocked to the side. "So, you already cancelled his upcoming appointments, then? After the attack?"

"Do you mind if I take a look at your ID?" Brynn asked. "I probably should've confirmed that you are who you say you are before letting you in."

Gemma gave a casual shrug.

"I don't have it on me. Sorry."

Her driver's license was in her wallet, in her back pocket, but she felt uneasy about letting this woman even glance at her home address.

Gemma walked quickly back down the hallway, with Brynn right behind her calling, "Wait. Miss Jaeger, please..."

"Really need to get to the hospital! Thank you for all

your help!" Gemma waved over her shoulder as she burst out of the office building's front doors and into the fresh air. She ran-walked to her car, half-expecting a dozen men with butterfly nets to come chasing after her.

Harmony Springs is weird. Brynn was weird. And something weird was definitely going on with Clay's business. Whatever it was, she doubted it was any good.

Could *Brynn* be the Fury? Workplace romances happened and often went wrong. Or maybe it was a client? Though, thus far, Gemma hadn't really seen any evidence that he had any clients. Whoever it was, maybe Dani was right and her inner Fury hadn't been awoken by the rage of a spurned lover at all. Money drove people to all sorts of madness. Could the Fury be a client whom Clay had harmed, or even ruined, financially?

As Gemma left Clay's office, she once again found herself with more questions than answers.

What the hell has this man gotten himself into?

It was time to find out everything Danielle knew about her husband's business, even if it did come across as prying. Even if Danielle took offense. It was relevant. And Danielle had to know more about the occupation of the man to whom she was married than she was letting on.

Gemma tried to imagine the conversation, right after Clay and Danielle moved to Harmony Springs and there were no openings at the police department for him.

I'm going to start my own business, Clay would've announced over a candlelit dinner for two.

Yay! Danielle would've said.

I'm going to be a consultant!

Yay! I'm so proud of you!

Gemma shook her head. No way. Danielle would've asked questions. Yes, love was blind, but Danielle wasn't stupid. She would have at least wanted to know what kind of consulting Clay was doing. Their parents did not raise them to just nod and smile and take whatever bull someone fed them as the gospel truth without digging further to sort facts from fiction.

Her sister would not be that naïve.

Dani had called her down here to investigate the attack on Clay. In order to do that, Gemma had to know the full story. Even if it was something that Danielle wasn't going to like telling her.

Gemma deliberately drove under the speed limit, watching each car passing her by.

The feeling that she was being watched was back, and it was making her skin crawl.

Her heart was pounding in her chest, and her breaths came in short, shallow gasps. Every time she turned a corner, she expected to see a figure lurking in the shadows, but there was never anyone there.

But she couldn't shake the feeling that Harmony Springs was anything but the quaint picture-perfect town it made itself out to be.

LIKE CLAY'S BUILDING, the Fish and Wildlife Services Office was on Main Street. All the businesses in Harmony Springs seemed to be on Main Street.

Once parked out front, Gemma got out of her Jeep and strode to the front door of the building, hoping it would be open.

Relieved that it wasn't locked, Gemma pushed the heavy wood door open. She stepped into a small, cramped waiting area with only a few plastic chairs and a coffee table. The walls were a pale green that needed repainting.

The linoleum floor was stained as if it had never had the pleasure of being introduced to a mop.

Gemma raised an eyebrow. *A chink in Harmony Spring's shining armor?*

"Can I help you?" a woman asked from behind the booth at the front. She wore a dark olive green uniform, as if she were some kind of soldier.

"My name is Gemma Jaeger. I'd like to speak to someone about my brother-in-law."

"Your brother-in-law?"

"Clay Smith," Gemma clarified. "I'm trying to learn if any headway has been made with his attack."

The woman's eyes widened slightly at the mention of Clay's name. "Oh, my. It's so terrible what happened to your brother-in-law, Ms. Jaeger. Let me get the agent looking into that matter for you. Please have a seat."

Gemma didn't want to have a seat. She watched the short buxom woman, whose nameplate read Sylvia, shuffle quickly into an office. Sylvia didn't close the door behind her, so Gemma could hear her voice, high and nasally, as she spoke to the man inside. Gemma didn't hear his response, but Sylvia responded with a series of dramatic hand gestures.

Though Gemma couldn't make out what Sylvia was saying, the officer inside wore an agitated expression, his face red. He his head back and forth, adamantly, as if he was refusing to come out and speak to Gemma.

Gemma wasn't offended. She'd rather have deal with a real person with real reactions than choreographed friendly waves and fake smiles. And she, too, would be agitated if she'd been sent on a wild goose, er, wild wildcat chase. Of course, he was getting nowhere on Clay's case and if she were in his shoes, she wouldn't want to speak with a member of Clay's family, either.

After a few moments, Sylvia walked back to her post behind the booth.

She flashed a smile at Gemma. A *fake* smile.

Ugh.

"Miss Jaeger, Agent Palmer will see you now," Sylvia gestured toward the office she'd just come from. "Go on in."

"Thank you," Gemma said, but uneasiness roiled in the pit of her stomach.

Gemma didn't miss Agent Palmer's eye roll as she approached. She also caught his curse as he moved to stand. Gemma gestured for him to sit, and he collapsed back in his chair. He returned the favor by extending his hand open-palmed, inviting her to sit as well.

His office smelled of cheap coffee and cigarettes, though Gemma saw no evidence of either. His bloodshot eyes, sandwiched between thick eyebrows and deep circles, observed her critically. It was clear that this man hadn't slept in days, yet still he had an air of authority about him. He was a man who believed himself righteous and important.

Noting the way his eyes never met hers and how he didn't even bother to offer to shake her hand, she surmised that power games were clearly this man's forte. He wouldn't want to admit failure. She would clearly have to let him lead if she was going to get information out of him. Men like this were easy. You just had to let them believe you fully accepted the fact that they were in charge.

"Thank you so much for taking the time out of your busy schedule to see me, Agent Palmer," she said, as sincerely as possible.

He held up a hand to cut her off mid-sentence. "Call me Palmer. We're not so formal around here. How may I help you today, Ms. Jaeger?"

"Well, like I said to Sylvia, is it?"

"Yes, Sylvia."

"Clay Smith is my brother-in-law. My sister is *extremely* upset about what happened to him."

"The whole town is, Ms. Jaeger. Harmony Springs is a tight-knit community." He sounded as if he was reading from a brochure.

Gemma waited for more, but nothing else came.

"Have you found what attacked Clay yet?" Gemma asked. "Certainly a man with your resources and experience must have figured it out?"

His brow furrowed. He swung his head slowly from side to side. "At this point, I have nothing for you. As I told your sister, as soon as I have any updates, I'll be in touch."

In other words, *Don't call me, I'll call you.*

But she had no intention of letting the visit be a total waste of time.

"Well, tell me this. Has there ever been this sort of attack in Harmony Springs before?"

"Frankly, I've only been here a short period of time, Ms. Jaeger."

"Oh," Gemma said, trying not to sound *too* intrigued by that nugget of info. "So, what brought you to Harmony Springs?"

"The guy who sat in this chair before me died suddenly, and they called me in as a replacement from out of state. But to my knowledge, no, nothing like the attack on Mr. Smith has ever happened here before."

"Ah."

"But I don't like it one bit, I'll tell you that. Harmony Springs is a peaceful town. That was one of the main reasons I decided to take the position. You know, for my wife. She wanted to get away from the city. The high crime rate was really starting to scare her. But now we gotta worry about mountain lions and such maiming innocent folks in their own yard? I assure you, I won't stand for it. No siree, I will not stand for it."

You're too busy sitting on your ass to stand for anything!

"So, what is the plan?" Gemma asked, suddenly overwhelmed by impatience and frustration. She clutched the armrests of her chair. "Are you going to wait on the guilty mountain lion to mosey on down and turn itself in or what?"

He stared at her for a moment, evaluating her, before leveling her with a serious stare. "Ms. Jaeger. Within fifteen minutes of being notified of the attack, I've had men on the ground, scouring the surrounding woods. I even have deployed a couple of guys up into the mountains. But right now, all they're coming up with are the typical foxes, rabbits, possums. Nothing large enough to attack a grown man and do the damage that was done to your brother-in-law."

It was times like these Gemma wished the world could just call a spade a spade. Yes, Hunters would always have to do the work, but their work would be far easier if the population at large could acknowledge and accept that the work *was* there to be done. Then Agent Don't-Call-Me-Agent Palmer could say, *Well, Ms. Jaeger, your brother-in-law wasn't attacked by any wild cat and, in fact, there seems to be something preternatural at foot and I am not the man for this job, so you take lead from here. Let's get some of the best Hunters you know to Harmony Springs, STAT. My men and I will cooperate in any way I can.*

But it was what it was. And as a result, what Agent Palmer said was, "I'm sorry that I couldn't give you anything else. But that's all we have right now."

Gemma nodded.

He would never admit it, but this guy was in *way* over his head.

"Okay, thank you for your time."

"No problem."

"Don't worry, we'll keep looking."

Thanks for nothing, Gemma thought.

She nodded. "Well, thank you for your time."

Gemma left Palmer's office and walked back to her car, hit with the overwhelming urge to *run*.

Get out of here as fast as you can! her brain screamed at her, but she kept a casual pace.

She scanned the area around her. The feeling of eyes on her skin was so strong it was as if someone was actually touching her. She pulled up the camera on her phone to see behind her as she walked until she got to her Jeep. Once inside, Gemma adjusted her rearview and side mirrors.

She saw no one.

But, once again, she couldn't shake the feeling that someone *was* there.

CHAPTER 8

On the way to the hospital, Gemma's focus was divided between watching the road in front of her and keeping a close eye out for any vehicle she may have noticed previously, making certain she wasn't being tailed. Not only did she not see any cars she recognized, she didn't see any cars at all.

Inside the lobby of Harmony Springs General, Gemma walked up to the front desk and patiently waited for the receptionist to finish her call.

"How may I help you today?" she asked Gemma, after hanging up.

Her smile was genuine. In fact, this woman was *beaming*.

"I'm here to visit my brother-in-law. Clay Hi—"

"So you've heard the good news!" the receptionist exclaimed, cutting Gemma off before she could correct herself.

"The good news?"

"Mr. Smith is awake!"

Gemma could've sworn there were happy tears in the receptionist's eyes.

Hmm. Wouldn't Dani have called to let me know if they were bringing Clay out of his medically induced coma?

"He's in room 308," the woman chirped, handing her a visitor's badge. "The elevator is that way."

Gemma ran—not walked—to the elevator.

But when Gemma got to Clay's room, she didn't go in immediately. She stopped outside and looked in the open door.

A lump formed in Gemma's throat as she watched Danielle with her husband.

Clay murmured something to Danielle as he held her face in his hands, tenderly wiping away her tears with his thumbs. She listened as Danielle told him over and over again he was going to be okay. That everything was okay now that he was awake. Seeing them together, when they thought no one was looking, made Gemma realize just how much Danielle did really love him. And it looked like Clay loved her just as much, if not more. In that moment, every cell in Gemma's body hoped she had been wrong about him, for her sister's sake.

But on the other hand, if Dani believed the *everything is going to be okay* spiel, she was delusional. Gemma hoped that Dani was putting on a front for Clay's sake. She could understand Dani wanting to do that... but they didn't have time for it now.

If news was quickly spreading that he'd regained consciousness, that was time to step up precautions, not lower their defenses. The Fury that attacked him might not feel compelled to finish the job while he seemed like he was on death's doorstep. She might just let nature take its course. But if it seemed he was recovering...

Danielle looked over and caught sight of Gemma in the doorway. She smiled at Clay as she patted his hand. Then she rose to make her way over to Gemma.

"He's awake!" Dani said, sweeping Gemma into a hug. "He's going to be alright!" Then she whispered in Gemma's ear, "Sheriff Dobbs came by and questioned him. He doesn't remember anything, other than being hit over the head from behind."

Gemma fought a groan.

Of course not. That would be too easy.

Dani let her go after a moment and pulled her into the room.

"Hello, Clay," she said. She sounded curt, but she couldn't help it. The animosity she felt every time she thought of him stayed at a constant simmer, and right now, in his presence, she could only focus on keeping it from boiling over.

"Hi, Gemma. Thank you for coming to take care of my girl while I was unable to," he said.

Gemma braced herself.

What would his next words be?

That now that he was awake, she could head on back to East Haven?

But his next words weren't directed at her at all.

Pleasantries exchanged, he turned back to Dani.

"I'm sorry to have worried you," Clay said to Danielle, his voice getting coarser. "I'm sorry about all of this."

What an odd thing to say. Unless, of course, he knew why he'd been attacked. Unless he knew he was to blame.

Gemma stared at him. *Do you really not remember anything, buddy? Or are you pretending in order to keep your own culpability hidden?*

Leaning over in her chair, Danielle laid her head on Clay's shoulder as he slowly stroked her hair. The moment was uncomfortably intimate. Gemma looked around the room to focus on anything but the unity and oneness she saw between them.

Danielle didn't need anyone but Clay.

"Shh," Danielle cooed as she stared deeply into his eyes. "It's not your fault that you were attacked. I won't hear it."

Ain't that the truth.

Clay began coughing. He struggled to sit up.

"No," Dani scolded him. "If you try to move, your stitches might not hold! You heard Dr. Jebran!"

"I need you to listen to me right now, Danielle. I need you to understand. What I'm about to tell you is extremely important."

"You need to rest," Danielle coaxed, trying to get him to lay back again. "And don't you worry about me. So you just hush and rest."

"Danielle—"

"I'm fine. I've got Gemma here. She's not going anywhere."

Gemma wasn't going anywhere. That was a fact. And *she* was listening, even if Dani wasn't.

Was Dani afraid of what Clay might say? That Gemma might be right about him? Was she trying to keep him from confessing?

"How is she going to help?" Clay asked. "The two of you don't even understand what is going on."

What?

Feeling dismissed and not willing to step aside so easily this time, Gemma looked him dead in the eyes, letting him know she meant business.

"I'm here as long as Danielle needs me to be," she said, glancing from one to the other. "I'm definitely not leaving her alone in that house. And the fact of the matter is, we know more than—"

"Gemma! Not now." Dani said sharply, cutting her off. "I

want Gemma here," Danielle nodded. "But even after you're released from the hospital, she's always going to be welcome in our home. She's our family, after all. Isn't that right, Clay?"

A warm feeling flowed through Gemma as she met her sister's eyes, but she didn't have time to enjoy it. Clay reached up and caught Danielle's arm in a death grip.

"Hey," Gemma protested, as Dani yelped.

Gemma was about to physically intervene, but Clay spoke again. The urgency in his voice paralyzed her.

"Danielle, you have to listen to me. I don't know how long we have."

"Oh, don't you dare talk like that, Clay! We have a life-time. Our best days are ahead of us. This was just a bump in the road."

But as if in disagreement with her, one of the machines Clay was hooked up changed from slow beeps at regular intervals to erratic *bonk bonk bonk bonks*.

A middle-aged nurse rushed into the room. "Page Dr. Jebran!" she yelled into the hallway over her shoulder.

"What's happening?" Dani's voice was frantic over the machine's panicking. "What's going on?"

"Miss, please step aside," the nurse ordered her as another nurse and an orderly swooped in, popping the rails on his bed up. But Dani refused to let go of Clay's hand, so they worked around her.

"Dr. Jebran will meet us in imaging," the second nurse informed the first.

"What is happening!" Dani demanded.

The orderly put up the rails on Clay's bed.

"I need to speak to my wife first," Clay protested, as they wheeled him toward the door. "Please give us a few minutes—"

"If you have a brain bleed, you may not have a few

seconds, Mr. Smith," the nurse said, bluntly, causing Dani to cry out.

"Danielle, please. Listen to me," Clay called. "No matter what, I need you to know I love you. I have always loved you. That wasn't a lie. No matter what else may have been, that part wasn't."

"What?" Dani whispered. "What are you talking about?"

"Gemma, I need you to PASS this WORD on. I will never forget our first HALLOWEEN together. I will ASK THE RISK. JAMES BOND is my favorite. I love your sister BACKWARDS and FORWARDS."

Danielle clung to Gemma.

"What is he talking about?" she asked, as if Gemma would know.

"I don't know," Gemma said. It all sounded like nonsense to her, but if one was suffering from a brain bleed, maybe speaking nonsense was standard? But there'd been such urgency in his voice, and the odd stressing of certain words.

Gemma committed it to memory, while holding Dani up.

Another nurse appeared. "Mrs. Smith, why don't you and your friend go down to the cafeteria to wait? I'll personally come and update you—"

"No," Dani said. "I'd rather stay in the room and wait on him if I can."

"That sounds like a good idea, Dani," Gemma said. "Let's go down to the cafeteria. You haven't had anything to eat today, have you? Neither have I so let's just go grab a quick bite."

"The cafeteria is—" the nurse began.

"I know where it is," Danielle snapped. "But at this particular moment, I don't have much of an appetite. Go get some pudding or something if you want it, Gemma. I need to walk around and clear my head first."

"I'll come with—" Gemma began.

"No," Dani said. "I want to be alone."

Gemma and the nurse exchanged a look, both thinking the same thing: That wasn't a really good idea.

She held her head high as she passed the nurse, then Gemma.

"Don't come after me, okay?" Dani asked.

"But Dani, we really need to talk about everything Clay just said back there—"

I have always loved you. That wasn't a lie. No matter what else may have been, that part wasn't.

"Don't," Dani said again.

She looked like someone who'd just lost her entire world.

Gemma didn't want to leave her, but she didn't want to lose her again, either, so it was important she play by Dani's rules, as infuriating as they were.

She couldn't ignore the fact that Clay had admitted he'd been lying. But what had he been lying about?

"You know what, I actually have a couple of calls I need to make, so I'm going to wait in the atrium on the first floor for some privacy," Gemma said.

This would give Danielle time to herself and give Gemma some time to consider everything Clay said before they took him away. "I'll look for you when I'm finished."

"Thank you," Dani whispered, with so much defeat and distraction in her voice that it made Gemma's heart clench.

Gemma made her way down to the atrium. As she'd walked from Clay's room to the elevator, she'd once again been overcome with the eerie sensation of being under the scrutiny of unseeing eyes.

Gemma found the atrium quickly enough. Which was good, because she didn't have a lot of time and she needed Randy to check out a few more things.

"Hello?" Randy's husky voice was both rough and gentle, like sandpaper wrapped in cotton.

"Randy, it's me again."

"Must be my lucky week. Another call from the one and only Gemma Jaeger? Did that information get you anywhere?"

"What I got is more questions." She could feel the frustration and anger welling up inside her, and she took a deep breath to try and calm herself.

"Yeah?"

Gemma quickly ran down everything she found and didn't find since she last spoke to Randy, starting with Clay's office, where no work actually seemed to happen, and ending with Clay's last words to her and Dani—which she hoped wouldn't be Clay's literal last words. Dani needed to know the truth, no matter what it was. Living with important questions unanswered was never-ending torture.

"What can I do to help, kiddo?"

"I don't know, Randy." Gemma exhaled. She wasn't sure if there was anything else he could do. "Tell me, am I out of my depth here? Am I too rusty from being out of the game? I don't see how I'm ever going to find the identity of the Fury. The only person I can think of it could be is Brynn and I'm only basing that on the fact that she's an attractive woman who knows Clay."

"Give me her last name. I'll do some digging there," Randy offered.

Gemma groaned. "I didn't get her last name."

God, her head hurt.

"Well. Not to be Mr. Insensitive, but if your brother-in-law doesn't make it, the identity of the Fury's fairly moot, isn't it? She'll have gotten what she wanted, so there won't be any need for her to come back."

"He seemed fine, though. I mean, he wasn't making any sense and the monitors were going nuts, but he was conscious."

"I hope you're right and they have him stabilized in a snap, but 'til that's the case, you just focus on being a good sister. That's more important than being a good Hunter right now."

"But Clay admitted to lying…"

"Maybe you should stop being a Hunter for a minute and focus on just bein' Dani's sister," Randy said.

He was right, of course.

She told him so and wrapped up the call. The stairs were closer than the elevator, so she took those.

Until they knew Clay was okay, she needed to make sure Dani was okay.

And judging from the ragged screams Gemma heard before she even pushed open the door leading from the stairwell to Clay's floor, Dani was anything but okay.

CHAPTER 9

"He's dead!" Dani's voice wailed. "He's dead! He's dead! He's dead!"

No!

Gemma found Danielle outside Clay's room, collapsed on her knees.

His door was closed.

All the doors to the patients' rooms were closed.

Danielle clutched handfuls of her hair, as if she was going to yank it from her scalp by the roots.

Racing to her sister, Gemma dropped to her knees, pulling Dani into her arms.

Hospital staff stood around, staring.

Gemma found the eyes of the first nurse who'd come into Clay's room, when the monitor had gone berserk. "What happened? Was it a brain bleed?" she asked, as Dani bucked in her embrace. She clearly didn't want to be restrained, but Gemma couldn't bear to let her go.

The nurse shook her head. "No, he—"

"He was stabbed!" Danielle's shriek pierced Gemma's ear. She struggled free from Gemma's hold and collapsed to the floor, her body wracked with sobs. "He was stabbed to death!"

What the actual fuck…

"I'm going to have to ask everyone to back up. Back up, please. No one leave the premises. I'm going to need to interview you all."

"Sheriff Dobbs!" a man in a white lab coat called. "Thank God, you made it so quickly. In here." Dr. Jebran lowered his voice but Gemma still heard every word. "He was stabbed eight times. By the looks of it, from a standard kitchen knife."

"I'll take it from here, Dr. Jebran," the Sheriff tipped his hat at the man. He glanced at Dani, then met Gemma's eyes. "Ma'am," he greeted her, "are you the wife?"

Yes, my husband was stabbed to death, and I'm pushing my own grief aside to comfort this random sad lady, Gemma thought, sarcastically. *What an idiot.*

Something troubled her deeply about the exchange, but she was too busy trying to keep Dani from banging her head against the linoleum.

"Have security stationed at the doors of the hospital," Dr. Jebran shouted to no one in particular. "And someone please attend to Mrs. Smith!"

"We don't have enough guards to cover even the main exits," someone muttered.

But Gemma was focused on Dr. Jebran's last orders.

And someone please attend to Mrs. Smith!

A nurse strode towards them. Noticing the syringe in her hand, Gemma positioned her body between the nurse and Dani.

"Sorry, but no," Gemma said. Then she said, "I'm actually not sorry at all. I'm not letting you jab my sister with an unknown substance—"

"It'll calm her down a bit, is all," the nurse said.

"We're going to decline," Gemma said.

"But Dr. Jebran recommends—"

"We are going to decline," Gemma said again, this time with a bit more heft to the words.

Gemma put a hand on Dani's arm, squeezing just below the elbow.

It got Dani's attention for a second, which was long enough.

"Dani, I need you to get up, right now, and walk with me," Gemma whispered in her ear. Gemma helped Dani sit up, then stand. Danielle's body was shaking, and she felt unsteady on her feet. Gemma wrapped an arm around Danielle's waist and pulled her close, shielding her from anyone else. "There we go. There are some chairs over there. Let's go sit over there."

"No!" Danielle screamed. She jerked away from Gemma. "Why would a Fury want to hurt him? To kill him? He's never harmed a fly!"

That outburst drew the attention of everyone within earshot. They all pretended to not notice. Gemma had to act fast before Dani said anything else that might get her locked in the mental ward of this hospital. This hospital which clearly was not safe. In a hushed tone, she murmured into Dani's ear, "We can't talk about this here. They'll think you're crazy talking about Furies."

Gemma put her hand on Dani's arm. Squeezed her elbow.

"How did it get in the hospital without anyone seeing it?" Dani went on. At least her voice was lower this time.

Besides, if Clay was stabbed, it most definitely wasn't a Fury attack.

Unless...

Perhaps the Fury had entered the hospital in her human form and, without her talons and razor teeth, had had to resort to using a weapon? Maybe it was someone who was already in the hospital when she heard Clay was awake and she'd grabbed a steak knife from the cafeteria…?

No.

Gemma knew better. She'd been trained better.

If Clay was stabbed, it most definitely wasn't a Fury attack.

A part of the Fury's vengeance was the viciousness of their rage. Their talons ripping the flesh from the bones of the person who'd wronged them. Their teeth plucking out organs and spitting them out like old chewing gum. The needed the dying as much as the death.

None of this made any sense. First, the Fury had attacked Clay, but hadn't killed him. Then someone had killed him, but it wasn't a Fury.

The bottom line was Gemma wasn't sure of anything anymore, including the killer's motive, especially since Clay had confessed to lying about… who knows what. Who knew how many enemies he had, or where they were, or if they would come after Danielle?

"Look. We can't talk about this here, Danielle." Gemma turned so she was facing her sister. She grabbed her by the shoulders and shook her gently, until Dani made eye contact. "Okay? Come on. Let's get you somewhere safe. You have to let your instincts kick in right now."

Dani shook her head, rivers of tears flooding her cheeks. "I can't," she whimpered.

"Remember what Mom and Dad always said. When you can't trust anything else, trust your gut. When you can't trust your gut, trust each other. Trust *me* right now. Whatever just killed Clay was *not* a Fury, but it *was* in this hospital. That means everything has changed. That means we both could be in danger. We have to get out of here. Now."

"B-bu-but…"

What do I say to get through to her?

The words sprang into Gemma's head in an instant.

"Dani. Clay told me to take care of you. Let me do that."

"W-w-we're not supposed to l-l-leave," Dani stammered.

"Well, Jaeger girls weren't raised to do what they were supposed to, now were we?" Her arm around Dani's shoulder, Gemma turned her, steering her towards the staircase. Could Dani make it down three flights? She doubted it. But Gemma would carry her piggyback if she had to. Trying to take an elevator would be too inconspicuous.

"Mrs. Smith!" a voice called.

Fuck it all to hell.

Dani glanced over her shoulder.

Had her sister lost all sense of self-preservation?

She just lost the love of her life. Give her a break, Gemma ordered herself.

"It's Dr. Jebran," Danielle sniffled, turning. Gemma followed suit as the doctor approached.

"Are you okay, Mrs. Smith?" he asked, causing Gemma to wonder how any of his patients could possibly trust any of his diagnoses. It was obvious Danielle was not okay. Her hands were fluttered like autumn leaves. Her eyes were red and wild with disbelief. She swayed slightly from side to side as if she needed to fall down, but her body couldn't decide which direction it wanted to go.

"She just lost her husband, Dr. Jebran," Gemma said, as politely as possible.

"Miss Jaeger, all things considered, I think it's best if we put your sister in a room for the night. I can give her a sedative. We'll let her rest. Sleep would be the best thing for her right now." The doctor's voice was soft and comforting, and he gave Gemma a reassuring smile. She appreciated his efforts, but they did little to ease the knot of fear that took up residence in her stomach.

Dani glanced at her, with big, questioning eyes.

Gemma had an unsettling case of déjà vu.

Nope. Not happening. They'd been there and done that with Peaceful Pines. But Gemma would never leave Dani in anyone else's care, ever again.

"There is no way I'm leaving my sister here," Gemma began, planting her feet firmly on the ground. Her hands came to rest on her hips. There was a steely determination in her gaze. "Her husband just died here of unnatural means. Until we know what happened to him, she is not going to be anywhere near this place."

"Mrs. Smith, I really think neither of you are thinking clearly at the moment and what you need—"

Quickly interrupting Dr. Jebran, Gemma looked Danielle in the eye. "I know what you need, Danielle. I will protect you. I promised Clay I'd take care of you, and I will."

Say something, Dani. Don't vanish inside yourself again. Don't leave me again.

"I know you will," Dani whispered.

Gemma nearly collapsed with relief.

"I'm sorry, doctor, but I'm taking her home," Gemma's voice was firm and resolute.

"Not so fast," a voice sounded behind them. "*I'll* decide who can leave and when and both of you have some questions to answer before you go anywhere."

CHAPTER 10

Gemma glanced over her shoulder.

It was the Sheriff. He was a towering, muscular man, standing at least six-four and weighing probably two hundred and fifty pounds or more.

His badge glinted in the fluorescent light.

"My condolences for your loss," he said to both of them. "I understand the victim is your husband, Mrs. Smith."

"Yes," Danielle said quietly. "And this is my sister, Gemma."

Danielle's eyes darted around the room as if she expected something to jump out at her.

"Gemma Jaeger," Gemma added as she shook the man's hand, giving it a bit of a squeeze to let him know she wasn't a woman who scared easily. His grip was firm, but she met his gaze head-on, not backing down. She would not be intimidated by this man. Not when her sister's life was in danger.

The Sheriff scribbled something down in his notebook.

"Sheriff," Gemma spoke, seeing Danielle was visibly beginning to shake. Her eyes were glassy and her lips had lost their color. "Is it necessary for this conversation to take place here? We're more than willing to answer any questions you might have for us, but I'd like to get my sister home."

"Apologies for the inconvenience, ma'am. I'm waiting for someone from the forensics team to arrive. I really need the answers while they're still fresh in your minds," he said. "Let's go to this alcove." He directed the sisters just ten feet away, to a semi-private area with semi-comfortable chairs. "I'll make this as quick as possible."

Danielle sat, her knees pulled to her chest and head slumped against them. Gemma sat next to her, taking her hand, and squeezing it.

Stay with me, stay with me, stay with me.

"Look," Gemma said, as respectfully as possible. "I know you need to get to the bottom of this, but I don't know how much more my sister can take."

Swinging his gaze toward Danielle, he said quietly, "I don't want you to think I don't sympathize, Ms. Jaeger, but a crime has been committed, and it's my job to get to the bottom of it."

Part of her wanted to sarcastically ask if his prime suspect was still a mountain lion. Perhaps if he hadn't turned the investigation over to Fish and Wildlife so quickly in the first place, Clay would still be alive and there wouldn't be another crime to investigate.

"It's okay, Gemma," Danielle said quietly as she lifted her head. "The sooner we answer his questions, the sooner we can leave. Right?"

"That's true," he agreed before noticing his team arriving. The sound of their footsteps and voices echoed in the hallway as they approached, but he held them off with an open hand. "I'll start with the basics. If I have any follow-up questions, you'll be called in."

"That's fine," Gemma said as Danielle nodded in agreement.

"Your husband was involved in a recent wild cat attack. Is that true?"

Gemma glanced at Dani out of the corner of her eye, praying Dani wouldn't decide to trot out the whole Fury theory now.

"Yes, that's why he was in the hospital."

Blowing out a breath, Sheriff Dobbs asked point-blank, "Is there anyone who would cause your husband harm?"

"No." Dani's voice was small, but sure. "No one."

"Mrs. Smith," the Sheriff continued. "I understand you had just left your husband's room."

"Yes, I did," She hesitated for a moment before continuing. "One of the monitors he was hooked up to started making a horrible sound. Nurses rushed in to take him for some kind of test."

"Imaging," Gemma said. "They said they were taking him to Imaging. Something about a potential brain bleed."

Dani whimpered.

The Sheriff nodded. "Yes. When they got him to the staff elevator, they realized a wire had come loose, causing the monitor to malfunction. Mr. Smith was fine at that point, so they brought him back."

Gemma knew what his next question was going to be before he asked it.

"Did either of you touch any of the medical equipment in Mr. Smith's hospital room?"

Gemma shook her head. "But I guess you'll know for sure once you dust for prints."

"I guess I will," he said.

"I touched his bed, but that's it," Dani said. She truly looked like she was going to pass out at any moment.

"And neither of you saw anything or anyone suspicious in or around the room before you left?"

"I didn't."

"Neither did I."

"And where did the two of you go when you left the room?" he asked the sisters, but his focus was on Gemma. His eyes were cold and hard. Under his gaze long enough, she might question her own innocence.

"I walked around for a few minutes, then I came right back. I went in the room to wait and…"

"So, you're the one who discovered the body?" Sheriff Dobbs asked Dani, even though she was gasping, as if she couldn't breathe.

"Could you be a bit more respectful?" Gemma demanded as Danielle began to sob. "Clay wasn't a body. He was her husband."

"And what about you, Miss Jaeger?" The detective fixed her with a steely gaze. "Where were you during the time of the suspected murder?"

"I went to make a personal phone call."

"And where exactly did you go to make that call?" he quickly asked, not taking his eyes off her. He raised his brows. His pen was poised over his notebook, ready to record her answer.

"I went to the atrium."

"I see," he said, taking down more notes. "Did anybody see you there?"

"Not to my knowledge," Gemma said.

"She wouldn't hurt Clay, Sheriff," Danielle defended Gemma. "You can't possibly think she's a suspect."

"Well, the way I see it, Mrs. Smith," he started, looking at Danielle. His eyes were sharp and calculating, like he was trying to determine the best way to strike. "From what

I hear, there's bad blood between your sister and your husband."

"Who told you that?" Dani asked.

"Are you denying it?"

"I'm neither confirming nor denying anything. I simply asked where you're getting your information," Dani said, getting a bit of her spunk back. Her shoulders were straight, her head up. "Because half the world doesn't get along with their in-laws. It doesn't make them murderers."

"I was only thinking that while your husband was vulnerable in the hospital, barely able to move... That would be an opportune time for someone to harm him. Obviously someone else had the same thought. And acted on it. Your sister is conveniently here. And I'm told they didn't get along."

By who?

Gemma was ready to knock this man on his ass. She really didn't like him, and her instincts were rarely wrong. Her fists were clenched at her sides, and she rose from her seat.

"Sit. Back. Down."

She obeyed, but only because Dani needed her by her side, not locked up in this Podunk town's one jail cell overnight.

"Look, did I dislike Clay? Yes. Did I dislike him to the point of killing him? No. I'm not a murderer, Sheriff Dobbs. But if I was? And I was going to take the opportunity to kill someone while they were in the hospital? I wouldn't stab them. There are plenty of ways I could've made it look like an accident and no one would have even suspected foul play."

"Is that right," Dobbs smacked his lips together. "Like tampering with his medical equipment? Attempting to inject something untraceable but lethal into his IV? Accidentally loosening a wire on the monitor in the process?"

Fuck.

She'd walked right into that.

"Maybe your brilliant Plan A went awry and you had to resort to Plan B?"

"Gemma would never kill Clay!" Danielle yelled. "Besides, she was never alone in the room with him before the monitor malfunctioned."

"I'm sorry, Mrs. Smith, but you must see it from my perspective. You've been living here for a handful of years, and the first time your sister is in town, your husband is attacked, and then killed? Awfully convenient if you ask me." The Sheriff's voice was heavy with skepticism as he turned to look at Gemma. She met his gaze head on, her own eyes flashing with anger and defiance.

She couldn't believe what she was hearing. Her mind reeled as Sheriff Dobbs' words sunk in. In one fell swoop, he'd pegged her as a duplicitous murderer. At least Danielle knew the truth. That was one thing Gemma could rely on.

"My sister was still in East Haven when the initial attack happened. That's why I called and begged her to come."

"Uh-huh," he said, doubtful. "How do you know she was in East Haven when you called her, though? Is it possible she snuck into Harmony Springs, attacked Clay, made it look like a wild cat, and then drove down the road a ways and waited on you to call her? Maybe she was only pretending to still be in East Haven while she was actually just at a motel down in Poplar Grove?"

The two sisters looked at each other. Then they both looked at the Sheriff as if he had grown a second head.

"You do realize how ridiculous that sounds, right?" Dani demanded.

"But if you want to go with that theory, my cell phone records will show you exactly where I was when Danielle called me."

That was logical, so of course, the bumbling Sheriff ignored it. "Now, if I'm correct, Mrs. Smith is your only living relative?"

"Yes, she is," Gemma said, even though she could feel the weight of his gaze on her and the pressure of his questions. Each felt like it was drawing her deeper into a maze she'd never find her way out of. But there was no point in denying facts.

"And you never called her before to come to see you, Mrs. Smith?"

"Clay suggested I wait until Dr. Downs thought I was ready," Danielle said, her voice low and steady. She stared at her hands, not looking at Gemma. The knuckles were drained of color, the skin stretched tight over bone. She looked like she was holding on for dear life.

Dr. Downs?

This was the first time Gemma had heard that name.

"My therapist," Dani said to Sheriff Dobbs, though Gemma got the feeling Dani was dropping that knowledge for her benefit, not his.

All this time, Gemma thought it was Clay keeping them apart, but in reality, it was an actual doctor who thought that her involvement in Dani's life could hurt her in some way? It gave Gemma a whole different view of the past few years. But what had Dani told Dr. Downs, to make Gemma seem like such a threat?

"Mighty big coincidence, though," Sheriff Dobbs went on. "Your sister shows up. Your husband winds up dead." He glanced at Gemma again. "You know this is the first homicide we've ever had in the history of Harmony Springs, Ms. Jaeger? Quite a coincidence indeed that it coincides with your first visit to our little utopia."

"That's it," Gemma snapped. Her anger was finally boiling over. She wanted to demand he do his damn job like he should've in the first place, and stop jabbing fingers in the air hoping he might accidentally point at the actual murderer. But she knew better. "We're not answering any other questions without a lawyer present."

"Gemmie," Dani began.

Sheriff Dobbs put away his notepad with a smug look on his face. "Look, we're not gonna get anywhere tonight. I see that now. You're both upset. I do need to advise you not to leave town, Ms. Jaeger. Neither of you."

"We won't," Gemma assured him. "We'll be at my sister's house."

First, she had nothing to hide, no need to run, as much as she wanted to get both herself and Danielle the hell away from Harmony Springs.

Second, she wasn't about to let another murderer get away scot-free and she had serious doubts that the Sheriff was going to be able to find the person who killed Clay.

"Good," the Sheriff said, standing, hiking up his belt, and heading back to Clay's room.

"You really shouldn't antagonize him," Danielle responded. "He is the Sheriff."

"Yeah, Sheriff Dumbass," Gemma remarked.

"Does that mean you're still on the case?" Dani asked.

"Dani," she said her sister's name as if it was made of the most fragile glass. "I can't track human monsters. You know that. I failed miserably with Mom and Dad's killer and—"

"Then I'll find them myself," Dani said through

clenched teeth. "I will not let them get away with taking Clay from me. I won't."

The venom in Dani's voice said she'd never give up. Ever.

Do you blame me for not finding Mom and Dad's killer? Is that why you really left me?

Gemma had never considered the possibility, but now…

"What I meant was, hell yeah, I'm still on the case," Gemma said, slinging her arm around Dani's shoulders. "I won't let whoever did this get away with it, Dani. I swear to you."

She could only hope Dani didn't remember Gemma making the same pledge to her about their parents' killer.

She'd failed miserably with that. But she wouldn't fail this time.

CHAPTER 11

"I can't go in there," Danielle whispered.

They were the first words she'd uttered since they'd left the hospital.

Her silence had terrified Gemma, even more than the thought of Clay's killer laying in wait for Dani or her or both of them.

Danielle sat in the passenger seat, not moving, her hands clasped in her lap. Gemma's hand rested on Danielle's knee. She gave it a gentle squeeze.

"Then you don't have to. We'll go to a hotel—"

"No!" Dani cried, grabbing Gemma's hand in a tight grip, keeping her from reaching for the key, still in the ignition. "I don't want to go to a hotel. We'd have to leave Harmony Springs. We can't do that, remember?"

There was panic in her voice, as if she thought Gemma was going to start the car, throw it in reverse, back out of the driveway, and take Dani away from Harmony Springs forever, never to let her return.

Though that is my plan as soon as we can make it happen, Gemma thought.

"The longer I put off going back in, the harder it'll be," Dani's voice trembled, but she'd adjusted her posture.

Her shoulders were back. Her head was held high. Her chin lifted, as if in defiance.

Tears streamed down Dani's face. It hurt Gemma's heart to know that though she could offer her sister temporary comfort, this would be a permanent heartache.

"What am I going to do without him?" Dani asked. "This was our home. How do I live here without him? This house will never be a home again."

She pressed a fist against her mouth, but was unable to suppress her sudden sobs. The sobs of a destroyed soul.

"You don't have to live here," Gemma kept her tone gentle, her words as neutral as possible. She twisted in her seat, pulling her little sister into an awkward sideways hug. "If you decide this isn't where you want to be, you can come back to East Haven with me," Gemma whispered. "You really can."

"This is where I'm supposed to be," Dani sniffed. The words sounded weepy but held a certainty that shocked Gemma.

"Even with Clay gone?"

Dani whimpered, as if she'd forgotten for a second and Gemma's question was a cruel reminder. But she nodded.

The sun was setting, turning the sky a deep red. The birds were singing their last song of the day. The wind blew through the trees, rustling the leaves.

Dani wiggled out of Gemma's arms. Though they were still sitting side-by-side, it felt like there was a quickly widening chasm between them.

What if she's slipping away again? What if I can't reach her? Clay was the one who brought her back last time.

Gemma would've never in a million years believed she'd long for her brother-in-law's presence, but for a fleeting moment, she did.

"I don't know how to explain it," Dani said. "But I belong in Harmony Springs. I *know* it."

Gemma's mind swirled with questions and concerns at Dani's conviction.

She's in shock. She's not thinking clearly.

"Let's go in," Dani said, suddenly. "I'm exhausted."

Helping Dani out of the car, Gemma walked her to the front door. She gently extracted her sister's keys from where they clinked together in Dani's shaking hands.

This is going to be too much for her.

"Look, you don't have to do this tonight. We can go find a room somewhere and stay for a few days. I'll bring you back, I swear, but I don't think you should stay here right now. You need time to heal, and this house is nothing but a reminder of—"

"My life with Clay," Dani interrupted, taking her keys back from Gemma, jamming the house key into the lock. "I'm going to stay here, regardless. This is my home. We were happy here. I'm not going to let anything drive me away from it. I'm not going to let the bad memories drown the good ones. I'm going to face all of them head on."

"Okay," Gemma agreed.

As far as Gemma was concerned, the conversation about where Dani needed to live was far from over. But Gemma knew she wouldn't get anywhere with Dani right now on that topic. Nor was it appropriate for her to try.

Dani pushed the door open. In the threshold, she inhaled deeply.

"Sooner or later, I'm going to forget the scent of him," she said, softly, sadly. "I wish I could bottle it."

"You won't forget," Gemma said, but standing behind Dani, still outside, Gemma shivered involuntarily. She automatically glanced over her shoulder, craning her neck in one direction, then the other.

She still felt like she was being watched.

Clay's killer is still out there.

But she didn't see anyone.

She squinted at Ms. Coffey's house.

The lights were on. The blinds were still, with no visible gaps.

Gemma realized that Dani had moved into the house. She was now standing in the middle of living room. Staring at the pictures of her and Clay, wiping at her eyes.

"How do you know I won't forget, Gems?" Dani's voice was small, scared.

Gemma swallowed hard. "After we lost Mom and Dad, every time I'd start to feel like I absolutely couldn't handle it, I'd focus on one thing I loved about them. I'd concentrate on every detail I remembered of, say, Mom's favorite outfits. How Dad's voice sounded saying certain words."

Dani glanced at her, brow furrowed. "That didn't make you miss them more?"

"It did back then," Gemma said. "But now, all those little things… they're comforting."

"Like Mom and Dad were gone, but you kept as many pieces of them as you could."

Gemma nodded. "Exactly like that."

What she didn't say was that she'd practiced the same memorization techniques with the things she'd loved about Dani, too, while Dani was hospitalized. Just in case.

Of course, after Dani chose to leave her, Gemma had bitterly regretted that. That's when she turned to booze, to forget.

"Thank you for sharing that with me, Gemma." Dani's eyes brimmed over with tears. "I think I'll try that."

Dani yawned. "But maybe not tonight."

The past few days had been so immensely taxing, her sister was clearly physically worn out. But her heart was shattered and that had a way of keeping one's mind going. Emotions and *what if*s keeping you awake, refusing to let sleep take you. Then there was the fact that Dani had found her husband brutally stabbed to death.

Still, putting her to bed seemed to be the best option.

Gemma hoped that Dani could drift off, and by some miracle, she wouldn't have nightmares.

"Why don't you go lie down? I can bring you some tea or—"

Dani shook her head. "I don't need anything."

Her face contorted with emotion.

Gemma knew she was thinking that she didn't need anything but Clay.

"Okay, then," Gemma said.

"You should go to bed, too," Dani said. "I'm going to leave my door open. And let's leave the light on in the hall, okay?"

Gemma nodded. "Of course. I love you, Dani."

"I love you, too, Gemmie."

"I need to call Matt, so I'm going to close my door. So I don't keep you awake for now. But I'll open it before I go to bed. And I'll check on you in a bit."

She waited on Dani to argue that that wasn't necessary, but Dani only gave her a melancholy smile.

Gemma went into the spare bedroom, closing the door behind her, so she could make that phone call. But— though she always wanted to hear Matt's voice—he wasn't the one she needed to talk to.

"How's Clay?" Randy asked, without even saying hello.

"Dead," Gemma replied.

She'd remained calm for Dani's sake, but now that she was out of her sister's presence, all her big sister bravado whooshed out of her. Her hands shook as she recounted the most recent events to Randy, and she could feel the fear rising in her throat.

"I don't think the danger's over. By far." She lowered her voice. "Clay's dead, but his killer's still out there. What if I was wrong about everything?"

"How so?"

"I can't shake the feeling that... I don't know. Killing Clay may not have been the main objective."

She had absolutely no evidence to support her claims. Her feeling was just a feeling. But Randy would believe her.

"I still feel like someone is watching me, Randy."

Randy sighed. "That's not good, kid."

"Tell me about it."

She was about to break the news to him that, for the time being, she was the Sheriff's most likely suspect when Randy said, "Hey, I know it's not the most convenient time, but while I've got you on the horn... I uncovered something I think you should know about while I was researching Harmony Springs. Can you handle me throwing something else at you?"

Gemma hesitated. Could she?

"It may not even be relevant. But then again..."

"If there's any chance it's relevant, tell me."

"So what I uncovered included a whole lotta medical jargon, so my interpretation may not be 100% accurate. But I think it's important. When infants are given their first vaccine, a blood test is also administered."

"Okay," Gemma said. *But what the hell did that have to do with Harmony Springs? There weren't any children here.*

"For a while, a vast majority of the labs were paid to look for a specific antigen in the samples they received. From there, any child that tested positive became part of the experiment."

"*All* of them?"

"All of them."

The thought of innocent kids—babies, from what Randy said—being used as guinea pigs made her sick to her stomach.

"Wait. Paid by who? What kind of antigen? What experiment? And what does this have to do with Harmony Springs?"

"It doesn't have anything to do with Harmony Springs, as far as I can tell," he paused, and Gemma's own blood ran cold. "But I believe it has quite a bit to do with you. Both you and Danielle were on the list of children tested."

"What?" Gemma asked, but no sound came out. "What were our results?"

"The thing is… It shows names of those tested. But not what their results were," he said. "But you and Danielle must've been negative."

"Why do you say that?" Gemma asked, not sure she wanted to know.

"The experiment involved a cure for the condition the antigen caused," Randy said.

"What condition?"

"I don't know, but Gemma, after several injections of the supposed cure… the children died."

Bile rose in Gemma's throat.

"Our parents couldn't have known about any of this, right?"

Randy hesitated. "I don't know. I dug until I couldn't dig anymore. Somebody didn't want this found. It was buried deep."

Gemma sighed. "Unfortunately, that's going to have to be a mystery to solve another day."

"Like I said, I didn't know if it was relevant or not."

"It's definitely interesting and something I'll look into

at some point. But thank you, Randy. I appreciate everything."

"It was no problem. Despite not being able to help you solve this thing, it felt good to try at least."

"Well, keep your phone charged. I still may need you."

"Will do."

As soon as she and Randy said their good nights—though this particular night had been anything but—Gemma felt incredibly alone.

She scrubbed her hands over her face and did the only thing she knew to do in moments where she felt completely unanchored to the world. She called Matt.

"Gems," Matt's soothing voice greeted her. "Everything okay?"

"No," she said. Her voice was thick with unshed tears. She couldn't manage to say anything more.

"Where are you? Let me come there. I'll throw a few things in a bag, and I'll be on my way in the next five minutes."

She couldn't let him get involved in any of this, but his eagerness to be there for her, with her, made her heart swell.

"No," she said. "No, that is completely unnecessary. I needed to hear your voice, is all."

"You *needed* to hear it, huh?" His voice was teasing.

She couldn't believe she'd admitted that out loud, but she was vulnerable and exhausted.

"Do you think you'll be home soon?"

"I don't know, to be honest." She bit her lip. Then she said, "Danielle's husband didn't make it."

She kept it vague. If she as much as uttered any words that indicated foul play, Mr. Reporter would be on his way, whether she liked it or not.

"Oh, Gems. Are you sure you don't want me to come?"

Did she want him to come? Yes. But it wasn't a possibility.

"Yeah. I need to focus on being there for Dani."

"Tell her I'm so sorry for her loss," Matt said. "I'm so incredibly sorry. If she needs anything. If I can do anything. You say the word."

He meant it. He'd never met Clay. Hell, he didn't know Danielle beyond what she was in elementary school. But he would do anything for Dani that Gemma asked him to. Without hesitation. Because he cared that much about Gemma.

Despite everything, the corners of her lips raised.

"Thank you, Matt. I appreciate…"

A noise outside caused Gemma's voice to trail off mid-sentence.

She waited a beat, silent and still.

Holding her breath.

Listening.

"Gemma. You still there?"

When she heard the sound again, there wasn't even a cell in her body that considered not investigating.

"Let me call you back," she uttered to Matt.

She ended the call and shoved her phone in her back pocket.

Her movements brisk and decisive, she snatched up the closest weapon. Her trusty crossbow. She couldn't stash it in her waistband, but it would have to do.

With her free hand, she eased the door open. Creeping out, she inched down the hall towards her sister's room. The light in the hall was still on. Dani's door was still open.

"Gemma, what the hell are you doing?" Dani hissed.

Gemma *shhh!*ed Dani, but there was that noise again, drowning her out.

This time it sounded like it was coming from *inside* the house.

Shit.

"Gemma!" Dani called again, her voice low but frantic. "Was that you?"

Quick and quiet, Gemma moved into Dani's room, crouching on the floor next to the bed. She placed her hand over Dani's mouth before Dani could scream. She couldn't risk Dani alerting the possible intruder to their whereabouts, but Dani immediately began to struggle.

"It's just me," Gemma whispered. "I think someone's in the house, though."

In the shaft of the light shining in from the hallway, the whites of Dani's wide, frantic eyes gleamed, almost supernatural.

Gemma removed her hand, thankful that Dani hadn't bitten a chunk out of her palm.

Before Danielle could say anything, Gemma put her finger on her lips to silence her.

Danielle nodded. She slipped out of her bed and knelt on the floor beside Gemma. The two moved alongside the dresser to the wall beside the door, staying low. Silent and stealthy, just like they were taught.

"Stay here," she told Dani, her voice barely audible, when they reached the doorway.

Dani was devastated. Distracted and depleted.

Gemma wasn't at the top of her game either, but out of the two of them, she was the one with a clearer head right now. She was their best shot at making it through this already tragic night alive.

Though she was out of practice, Gemma was a trained Hunter with excellent hearing and cat-like stealth. Two skills that led her to the intruder while he remained completely unaware of her presence. A beam of moonlight illuminated the kitchen, silhouetting the profile of a man who stood in the corner of the kitchen, where the two countertops met.

Gemma squinted, trying to make out some distin-guishing feature, but it was too dark. Besides, she was far more interested in what he was doing than who he was. He opened a drawer. She waited to see what he would take, hoping she would be able to tell what it was.

What are the odds this is a run-of-the-mill burglar and not Clay's murderer? Gemma wondered as she watched.

But the man didn't *remove* anything.

Instead, he reached inside his coat and pulled out a knife.

Gemma watched, slack-jawed, as he slipped the knife into the open drawer. She could've sworn he chuckled as he closed the drawer again.

He nodded.

Then he turned around.

She waited on him to take a step in any direction, hoping he'd choose hers.

He took a few steps with the swagger of someone who'd gotten away with something.

Even in the dark, she could tell he was pleased with himself.

Until he looked up.

Her hand had found the switch on the wall and rested on it, waiting for this exact moment.

Suddenly, the kitchen was flooded with light.

Gemma and the intruder were staring each other dead in the eyes.

"Fancy meeting you here. I'm assuming that knife you just planted was the one you used to kill my brother-in-law?"

CHAPTER 12

Agent Palmer froze.

Then, with reflexes too fast for someone who spent his days issuing fishing permits and setting out traps for bobcats, the so-called Federal Wildlife Officer's hand shot out, making a grab for the gun Gemma had anticipated he'd have holstered.

She was impressed by his speed, but it was no match for her own.

His wrist was pinned to his chest before he even registered the fact that she'd fired an arrow at him.

He bellowed.

"Take another step and I aim the next one at your femoral artery... and I never miss my target," she warned.

"You bitch," he spat out.

And the bastard took another step.

"Warned you," Gemma said, as the next arrow struck him, sending him to his knees.

"You missed my femoral artery," he gasped, trying to smirk like the cocky dumbass he obviously was.

Gemma strode toward him and crouched down, simply watching as the agony coursed through his body. "By less than two inches. But only because I'm not going to give you the privilege of bleeding out 'til you give me some answers."

He shook his head. But the tears in his eyes were about to spill over.

"Fine," she stood. "We'll do it your way."

Before he saw it coming, she swung her foot out, driving the second arrow further into his thigh, eliciting a howl.

"That was for bleeding on my sister's floor," she said. "Unless you want to find out what the punishment is for not answering every damn question I ask you, I suggest you start talking."

The color drained from his face.

"You killed my sister's husband and then you brought the murder weapon here to frame her for it. Why?"

He laughed. He coughed up some blood when he laughed, but he laughed. The blood dribbled down his chin.

"Not framing her. Framing *you*," he said, then he spit a mouthful of blood in her face.

She reached up and dragged her sleeve across her cheeks, as if it was rainwater she was wiping away. "You'd be unconscious right now if you didn't have info I need. So let me be clear. You can answer my questions and I might get you help. Or I can wait 'til you die, go grab a few hours shuteye, and deal with your corpse in the morning."

Unafraid of him getting hold of her, she yanked the arrow out of his arm. The open wound gushed, accentuating her point. As soon as he lifted his hand, she kicked him in the stomach, sending him flying back a few feet. He hit his head on one of the lower cabinets.

"Why did you kill Clay?" Gemma demanded. "And why did you want to frame me for it?"

"Because unlike your pussy-whipped brother-in-law, I

follow my orders. If he'd done what he had to do, neither of us would be having this conversation." His voice was heavy, weighed down by sadness and grief. As if he was already grieving himself. Knowing he'd die here, that it was his only option. "I did what I had to do. I can't tell you anymore."

Orders?

"What were Clay's orders?"

"To kill your sister," Palmer snarled.

"You're lying," Dani's voice was sharp, like a blade slicing through the air. Gemma hadn't even realized Dani had snuck into the room behind her. "Gemma, he's lying!"

When Danielle said the word *lying*, Clay's words came back to Gemma.

No matter what, I need you to know I love you. I have always loved you. That wasn't a lie. No matter what else may have been, that part wasn't.

"Dani, get out of here," Gemma said, in a warning tone.

Palmer groaned in pain before grinding out his next words, addressing Danielle, over Gemma's shoulder. "He fucked up the first time he fucked you, lady. Fell in love with his mark."

Gemma positioned her body between Palmer and Danielle, just in case her sister decided to lunge at him. Pummel him with her fists. Strangle him with her bare hands. Rip his face off. All things he deserved, but not yet.

Gemma could see the beads of sweat forming on his forehead. His shirt was soaked with blood. His eyes darted around the room, looking for an escape he knew didn't exist. Soon, he would fade without any further intervention.

"Who was Clay working for?" Gemma demanded.

Danielle screeched. "You don't believe him, Gemma!"

"Dani, stop!" Gemma snapped. If Dani couldn't see how important finding out as much as they could now was, Gemma would have to deal with her later. The fact that they'd never found their parents' killer ate away at Gemma every single day. Dani might not want all the details right now, when everything was so fresh and raw, but after she'd mourned Clay, the truth would matter to her. She wouldn't only want to know who was behind his death, but how and why.

Dani's priorities weren't straight right now, and Gemma didn't expect them to be or blame her for that. But Gemma's had to be.

"Please. I have a wife." Palmer's eyelids were growing heavy, as was his breath. Each one more ragged than the last. "At least let me call her. Tell her goodbye."

"You didn't give my sister the courtesy of letting her say goodbye to her spouse, so no, I don't think you deserve that."

"She's innocent. Hickman wasn't. Your sister isn't."
Hickman.

An inhumane noise escaped Danielle's throat, but Gemma couldn't take her eyes off Palmer.

He'd referred to Clay as Hickman. Everyone in Harmony Springs supposedly knew Clay and Danielle as the Smiths.

The heel of Gemma's boot connected with Palmer's knee, causing him to whimper.

"Dani is a victim in all this and if I hear you say otherwise again, your death will become a lot more slow and a helluva lot more painful."

"Please," Palmer begged. Gemma had to lean in to hear him now. "I'll tell you whatever you want to know. If you let me tell Irene I love her one last time."

Gemma shook her head, knowing better. There was no

Irene. Whoever this man so badly wanted to call… it wasn't a beloved wife.

"First you spill. Everything. Starting with who gave the orders. Was it the Sheriff?"

"You really think Dudley Do-Right is some kind of mastermind?" He barked a laugh. More blood dripped from his tongue with every word.

Gemma had to give him credit. He was hanging on way longer than she'd believed he could. Most men would've passed out from the pain after the second arrow, if not the first.

"It's a covert organization, lady. I only know who my direct orders came from. And they only know where their direct orders come from. And so on."

"So, your direct orders came from Clay, and you took him out so you could take over his failed mission and move up in the organization?"

But that didn't make sense. If Palmer had planned to head from the kitchen to Dani's room, to kill her, why not use the same knife, and *then* wipe it down, and put it in the drawer, pinning both murders on Gemma?

"You're making me wish I was dead, you stupid, stupid girl." Palmer coughed. He tried to draw in a breath but wheezed instead.

Danielle made that god-awful noise again.

I'm not going to get anywhere with this line of questioning.

"You killed Clay. But who originally attacked him? Was that you, too?"

Yes, *that* made sense. Palmer had attacked Clay and made it look like a wild cat had done it. That would mean he would oversee the investigation, not the Sheriff. He wouldn't have to deal with any other law enforcement poking around, looking for answers. There had never been a Fury.

Yet...

There *had* been Fury claw marks on the house.

Something still wasn't right. She was missing something.

"Have you been the one watching me?" Gemma demanded.

"W-w-what...w-w-atchin-ing. N-n-no."

A gurgling noise came from Palmer's throat.

Well, that wasn't good.

"I'm dying," he rasped. "You can't let me die."

"And you called *me* stupid?" Gemma asked. She wasn't heartless. If this had been any other circumstance, she would feel guilty that this man had summoned some faint sliver of hope that she'd pardon him. But she had no pity for this man who'd planned to murder her sister. He'd messed with the wrong family, and he was about to find out just how deadly his mistake had been.

But it was she who'd made the mistake.

Despite his blood-stained teeth and shirt, despite the fact that he already had the pale skin of a dead man, all the life was not gone from Palmer. Gemma still didn't know what organization he worked for or what kind of training he'd had, but he *was* well-trained. Before she'd noticed him move his good hand, it was wrapped around her ankle. Gemma tried to step back. She might've freed herself from his weakened grip, if there hadn't been blood on the floor. But she slipped and was falling. Her body crashed next to his. Her head banged against the tile. For a second, she saw only blackness, stars swimming behind her eyelids. When she regained her sight, she assumed the large shadow in her peripheral vision was her eyes playing tricks on her.

You've got to get up. You've got to fight him. Damnit, Gemma! Your mother and father didn't train you to go out like this!

But she was flat on her back, the wind knocked out of

her. Her out-of-practice, out-of-shape body betraying her in a way it hadn't ever done before.

As soon as this was all over, she'd start physical training again, sticking to the same regimen her family had when they were all hunting together.

But first she had to make it out alive. And make sure Dani made it out alive.

Suddenly, an ear-piercing shriek yanked Gemma's hazy attention from the ceiling, from the future, and back into the here and now.

She knew that high-pitched shriek. She'd never heard it in real-time, but she'd heard it many times on the training tapes their father made them listen to over and over.

There was another shriek, and this one was accompanied by the sound of the windows in the room shattering.

Gemma shielded her face from a few shards of glass.

With a loudly beating heart, Gemma turned her head. She blinked and saw exactly what she expected to see. Her eyes went wide, anyway.

She felt Palmer go slack next to her.

The creature rose to a full eight feet in height, its bald head brushing the ceiling.

Its large eyes were bottomless black, like two pits of darkness that could absorb one's soul, leaving nothing but a husk of skin where a life had once been. Its teeth were like daggers with razor-sharp points and edges. It had no hands—but claws with talons like scythes designed with the sole intent of drawing blood. The bat-like wings on her back unfurled. Her whip-like tail swished back and forth.

Before Gemma could even think of collecting herself, the Fury crouched and charged at her on all fours. One of its powerful limbs struck her side.

Was that sound a rib cracking? she wondered before she even registered the blinding pain. Instinct kicked in and she lifted her arms, striking one elbow out, hoping to get at least a jab in. Put up some sort of pitiful fight. But then she realized the Fury's blow hadn't been intended for her at all. She'd been collateral damage. In the wrong place at the wrong time. In between the Fury and its true target.

Gemma watched in silent horror as the Fury pounced on Palmer. With a swift downward motion, her middle talon sliced through Palmer's jugular. The man's neck became a fountain of blood.

The Fury hunched over him, tilting her head from side to side, transfixed as he began to twitch.

Danielle, Gemma thought, desperately.

At the risk of the Fury turning her attention onto Gemma, Gemma rolled over onto her side with a wince, looking around for her sister. Those terrible noises Danielle had made. Had Gemma been so intent on getting answers from Palmer, she'd let the Fury get to Danielle without even noticing?

She'd never forgive herself for that.

She saw no trace of Danielle. Or Danielle's body.

Without glancing back at Palmer or the Fury, Gemma kept her every movement minute. Her only hope was that the Fury was in a hypnotic state, enjoying watching as the life drained from her prey. Gemma did a shimmy-crawl toward the hallway on her elbows and belly.

She had almost made it when she heard Dani sobbing quietly.

She's alive. No matter what, she's still alive.

Her sister had somehow gotten away. Hid. Kept herself safe.

Gemma's relief was fleeting.

The sound wasn't coming from in the hall or one of the bedrooms or even the living room.

It was coming from behind her, back in the kitchen.

A bolt of energy shot through Gemma.

She leapt to her feet and whipped around.

There was no sign of the Fury.

There was only Palmer. His mouth was opened in silent scream. His eyes bulged with the terror of what he saw in his last seconds. He was dead.

And then there was Danielle, huddled against the cabinets. She looked like she'd barely escaped a war she'd been ill-prepared to fight.

"Dani, where'd the Fury go?" Gemma asked, her voice tight.

Gemma's chest felt like it was caving in. Dani's pupils were dilated, making her brown eyes appear completely black. Gemma's gaze travelled down, to Dani's blood-covered hand.

The Fury hadn't gone anywhere.

She had transformed back into her human form.

Danielle.

CHAPTER 13

No. Not Dani. It wasn't possible.

Stunned, Gemma inched backwards away from her sister, until her back was pressed against the opposite wall. She hadn't even thought to retrieve her crossbow from wherever it had wound up in the fray.

"Gemmie?" Dani asked like a scared child, who'd just woken abruptly from a nightmare. She looked over at Agent Palmer and gasped. Letting out a little help, she scrambled to get away from him. Her eyes met Gemma's. "What did you do to him?"

Gemma held up her hands, as if proclaiming innocence. "Dani, Agent Palmer broke in. Don't you remember?"

Dani shook her head back and forth slowly. She blinked up at Gemma, disbelief in her eyes.

If you have a hard time with that part of the story, just wait 'til you hear the rest, Gemma thought.

Gemma knelt down, so she was eye level with her sister. "What is the last thing you remember?"

Dani's eyes strayed to Palmer once again. "Even if he broke in, look at him, Gemma. We don't kill humans. Look at him! Those are your arrows, Gemma! You incapacitated him and then you carved him up!" Her voice got more hysterical with every syllable.

Fuck. If Dani wasn't going to listen to her, there was going to be hell to pay when the Sheriff ambled up.

Gemma was pretty sure he already believed she'd stabbed Clay to death.

He could easily make up a theory that would sound plausible for her to have murdered Agent Palmer. She'd lured Palmer here with a panicked call about another mountain lion sighting. Then he'd come up with some inane motive. She not only hated Clay, but she hated everyone in Harmony Springs, because she saw everyone in the town as having a part in taking Dani away from her.

"Dani," Gemma said again, this time her voice firm. She said her sister's name in the precise tone their mother would've used in this situation. That got Dani's attention. "What is the last thing you remember?"

"I went to bed. You were going to your room to make a call."

No, no, no, no, no.

Dani remembered none of it?

Glancing around at the room, taking in the destruction that had been done, Dani's eyes welled with tears. "Why would you do this to our home?"

Then Dani glanced down at her hands. She screamed and scooted back, as if she could run from her own body somehow.

"Danielle," Gemma said, very softly, very gently.

She didn't want to threaten Dani by grabbing her crossbow, but she needed to be ready to protect herself in case Dani's vengeance flared up and she transformed again.

No.

Even if that happened, even if Dani came after her,

she wouldn't fight it. She couldn't. Even if it was self-defense. She wouldn't do anything to hurt her sister. Ever.

"Dani," she said again. "The Fury was back. Look at how the windows are shattered. The Fury's shriek did that. Look at the wound on Palmer's neck. It's sliced open, like you said. The Fury's talon did that. Yes, I shot him with my crossbow, but the Fury killed him."

Danielle's eyes scanned the room, as if she was looking for any plausible evidence that what Gemma said is true. "Where did she go?"

Gemma closed her eyes. She took several deep breaths.

"It was you," she said, her voice barely a whisper. "You're the Fury, Dani."

"What?" Dani's voice was shrill.

"One minute you were here, in the room, with Palmer and me. The next minute, he and I got into a scuffle and you were gone. I thought you ran and hid, but then… The Fury was here."

"No, you're wrong. I don't believe you!" she cried, bewilderment in her voice. "Did you see me change?"

Gemma shook her head.

"But the Fury attacked Palmer. I crawled toward the hall to find you." Gemma swallowed, her throat bone dry. She gestured toward the hallway. "I thought you'd gone to hide in the bedroom. Then I heard you sob. I turned around and you were… right there. Right where the Fury had been."

Dani sniffled, tears streaming down her cheeks. "No. It's not possible. That means I killed Clay. That means…" her voice broke off into a tortured sob. She shook her head, furiously.

"Dani, no… Not only did you not kill Clay, I think you were trying to protect him…" The words spilled from Gemma's mouth faster than she could think them through.

"Just like tonight, when Palmer came after me. You were protecting me. Palmer killed Clay, not you. You were protecting him. Your vengeance was directed at Palmer, not me, not Clay."

"Why was Agent Palmer here?"

"He murdered Clay," Gemma said, softly. "He came here tonight to plant the knife he used to stab him. To make it look like I did it. And he was behind the original attack, as well. He made it look like a wildcat so that Fish and Wildlife would investigate instead..." Gemma let her words die on her lips.

She heard a door creak open.

Her ears perked up.

The front door.

Someone *else* was here.

"Do not move," Gemma whispered to Danielle. She was tempted to march into the living room and confront whoever it was, but like Dani, she likely looked like she'd been through hell. She had Palmer's blood all over her. Instead, she stood still, listening. Odds were it was either Sheriff Palmer, with an arrest warrant or... Maybe the organization Palmer claimed to work for somehow knew he'd been taken out of the game, and they'd already sent in a replacement?

"Yoo-hoo," a voice called.

"It's Ms. Coffey," Dani hissed.

"Ms. Coffey, it's really not a good time!" Gemma called, trying to sound pleasant.

But what was Danielle's elderly neighbor doing dropping by for a visit at this time of night? And didn't people in this godforsaken town believe in knocking?

"How are we going to explain—"

Before Danielle could get her question out, Ms. Coffey strode in.

"Now, now, I told you to call me Addie," Ms. Coffey said.

Gemma's mouth dropped open. Her eyes widened in shock.

The hunched back was gone. The cane was gone. In their place was a poised and defiant-looking older woman with perfect posture. Not a single age spot. Not a single wrinkle.

"What the hell," Gemma muttered.

Was everything in Harmony Springs a façade?

"What the hell indeed," Ms. Coffey echoed, surveying the scene. Then she glanced at Gemma with a kind expression. "It looks like you girls have had quite the evening."

Gemma glanced at Danielle. Danielle glanced back at her. Neither was going to jump to be the first to volunteer that they could explain. After all… they couldn't.

Ms. Coffey looked at Agent Palmer with a dismayed sigh.

"Miss Coffey, I—" Danielle began.

"Addie."

"Addie, I—"

"I assume Agent Palmer was here to do you girls harm?" Addie asked.

Gemma nodded. "But… why are *you* here?"

"Young ladies, the time has come for us all to drop all pretense. I heard the shriek. The unmistakable shriek of a Fury." Addie righted a chair that had toppled and sat down. With her hands in front of her in a surrendering expression, she crossed one leg over the other. "Gemma, did you see it happen?"

How the hell did old Ms. Coffey know Furies actually existed, let alone what they sounded like?

Gemma fought to keep her expression neutral. "Did I see what happened?" Her voice wobbled. Damnit.

"Did you see Danielle transform? Do you know what she is?"

Gemma felt lightheaded.

"Sit." Addie stood and gestured for Gemma to take her chair. "Now, it's very important for us all to remain calm."

Addie walked to Danielle and knelt beside her on the ground. She reached forward, one finger tracing the curls of Danielle's hair. "My poor child, you were not ready to hear the truth."

"The truth?" the sisters asked in unison and then looked at each other.

"You know the truth?" Gemma demanded. Then she softened her voice. Because, yes, if Dani was a Fury, keeping her calm was paramount. "*You* know the truth, Addie?"

Addie nodded. "And ready or not, it's time for the two of you to know it, as well. All of it."

CHAPTER 14

BEFORE SHE WOULD TELL THEM ANYTHING, MS. COFFEY—
Addie—had both Gemma and Danielle clean up and
change clothes. She had Dani take some sedatives Dr.
Downs had prescribed for her. Then she relocated their
small group to the living room.

"Long, long ago," Addie began. "A very wealthy
doctor's wife had an unfortunate encounter with a male
Fury. After that, the doctor became obsessed with Furies."

Dani shot her a look that didn't say, *Here I am, being
calm. No worries.*

Gemma pressed her lips together.

Addie went on. "The doctor discovered that certain
individuals had a genetic predisposition to *furia transformationem.* Loosely translated, Fury transformation. He closed
his plastic surgery practice. Opened a lab. Vowed to devote
the rest of his life to ferreting out Furies and… taking care
of the problem."

She'd thought what Randy had discovered about the
experiments and testing on children… the testing done on
her and Dani… would be another mystery for another day,
that it was irrelevant. But suddenly, it seemed extremely
relevant.

Gemma responded quickly, her eyes alight with understanding, "That's the antigen the blood tests were checking for, for the predisposition to *furia transformationem.*"

"How did you know about the tests?" Addie asked in quiet amazement, her voice barely above a whisper.

"What are you two *talking* about?" Dani demanded.

"Take deep breaths, love," Addie reminded Dani in a serene voice. She watched her for a moment. Once she seemed convinced all was well, she continued, "Some individuals possess this gene that, when triggered by extreme feelings of vengeance, will ignite a state of *Furia transformationem.* Dani, darling, you are one of those individuals."

Dani shook her head. "What does that mean? What's going to happen to me?"

"Absolutely nothing," Gemma reached over and took Dani's hand, but it was hard not to imagine it turning into a taloned claw.

Then Gemma turned to Addie.

"How do you know all of this?" Gemma asked.

"After a test was developed to find the antigen… Anyone who tested positive…" Addie broke off, unable to continue looking either of them in the eyes. "They were supposed to die in childhood."

Fear shot through Gemma. Ironically, unadulterated fury shot through her, as well.

Children were being killed to keep the Fury population to a minimum.

"Then I *can't* be a Fury. You said so yourself. I wouldn't be alive. Right?" Dani demanded.

"You *did* test positive, Danielle. You are predisposed to *furia transformationem.*"

Gemma kept her fingers intertwined with Dani's, keeping her tethered at her side. Dani's free hand flew to her mouth.

"Gemma did not. Once your parents were notified of your results, they didn't do what they were supposed to do, Danielle. They were supposed to have you 'treated'," Addie did air quotes around the word.

Dani whimpered. Or maybe it was Gemma herself.

"They didn't even consider it," Addie shook her head. "Not for a single second. They refused."

"And the doctor just let that go?"

"Well," Addie said, "he couldn't force anyone to do anything. He could only give his *strong* recommendations."

Gemma opened her mouth but before her questions could pour out, Dani spoke.

"So *am* I a Fury?" Dani's voice was raised, high, trembling.

Addie leaned forward and put her hand on Dani's knee. "No, love. You are not a Fury. You have the ability to transform into a Fury. But that's not who you are."

"Did you know she transformed on the night of Clay's attack, too?"

Addie nodded. "I did. I heard the shriek, as I did tonight. When I went outside, the Fury was in the air, chasing off Clay's assailant. He ran into the woods, so I didn't get a good look. I'm assuming it was Palmer?"

Gemma nodded.

"I suspected Palmer was up to no good from the moment he rolled into town to replace Agent Powell. But then again, we're always suspicious of strangers."

"Gee, I hadn't noticed," Gemma said with more than a touch of sarcasm. Gemma couldn't resist asking, "Has it been you that's following me around town, watching me?"

Addie looked genuinely perplexed. "Darling, we're wary around strangers, but we don't stalk them about."

Hmm.

Gemma was sure someone had been stalking her about. But maybe despite his denials, it had been Palmer.

"But I thought a Mr. Owens was the first one to come out after Clay's attack?" Gemma asked, shifting the subject again. "And that Dani was inside."

Addie nodded. "After Palmer got into the woods, Dani transformed immediately. Poor dear was so dazed. Recalled nothing. I brought her back indoors, sang her a little lullaby and, boom, she was out like a light. Then I slipped back out. Mr. Owens was already tending to Clay so I scurried back to my house to keep an eye on things from my window. I like to do that. A few minutes after the ambulances arrived, Dani came out."

"So that's why I remember hearing the Fury… because it was me," Dani looked equal parts awed and horrified.

"It's rare that a human with *furia transformationem* has any recollection of what happens during their shifted state, but I suppose it's possible," Addie said.

Gemma had other questions, pressing questions, but she wasn't sure if they were questions she should ask in front of Dani.

But Dani asked for her. "But why did Agent Palmer attack Clay in the first place? And why would he want to frame Gemma for it?"

Addie pursed her lips. "I can't say with any certainty, dearheart."

"Palmer said he had orders. Because Clay didn't follow through on *his* orders."

"Wait, what? What orders? What are you talking about?" Dani demanded.

Addie put her hand over her heart. "Oh, dear. They've found us. How is it possible? Unless Clay told Palmer…"

"Hello," Dani waved her arms. "Fury in the house. Don't make me transform on y'all's asses. Addie, you said it was time for us to know the truth. Tell me the damn truth. All of it."

Gemma watched as a forlorn expression crossed over Addie's face. Her eyes drooped and the corners of her mouth turned downwards.

"Clay *was* sent to kill you, Danielle," Addie said in a pained voice.

"What?" Danielle asked, her voice laced with shock and horror. She shook her head. "No."

Gemma focused on Addie with a hard stare, trying to get her attention, trying to ask with her eyes if this was really a conversation they needed to continue.

"Yes, darling," Addie said. "I'm sorry to be the one to tell you, but it's true. The night your parents were killed… the night you were attacked. It was Clay. He wasn't meant to kill your parents, only you."

Though well aware she wasn't predisposed with the Fury gene, Gemma could very well imagine herself transforming in that moment.

"That son of a bitch," she said under her breath as her lip twitched into a snarl.

"Your parents tried to stop him," Addie continued.

Pieces of the sick, twisted puzzle were finally clicking into place now.

"And that son of a bitch killed them." Gemma shook her head. "Which is why I never found the murderer. The only other person helping me search *was* the murderer."

All those years she'd searched. All of the dead ends she'd followed. And the murderer was right under their nose the entire time. Likely laughing as he sent her on wild goose chase after wild goose chase.

Gemma glanced at Dani.

"I think I'm going to be sick." Dani clamped a hand over her mouth.

Gemma felt like she, too, was about to vomit. Every bad vibe, every whisper from her gut, had been right. *She* had been right. Clay'd been the bad guy she'd suspected him to be for so long. But she'd never, ever suspected he could be such a monster.

"But…" Dani whispered. "He didn't kill me. He attacked me, but he didn't kill me. Why?"

"After Clay he was assigned to kill you, he spent months surveilling you, watching you. He developed quite the unhealthy obsession with you. But in the end, that unhealthy obsession saved your life. He couldn't kill you."

"Yet he kept coming back and looking for opportunities to finish the job, right?" Dani asked. "That's why he visited me when I was hospitalized? And then, afterwards, once he'd gotten me to fall for his charms… he got me to marry him. He convinced me to come here. He isolated me from my sister. Was our entire relationship a giant game of cat and mouse to him? Did he want to just drag it out and play with me as long as he could? Was he planning on killing me all along, just waiting for the right time?"

He fucked up the first time he fucked you, lady. Fell in love with his mark.

Gemma remembered the remark Palmer had made to Danielle, even if Danielle did not.

She hated Clay with every fiber of her being. She always would. He robbed her of her parents. But anything that would give Danielle even a small sliver of solace right now… Gemma would swallow all of her hatred and hand it over freely.

She shook her head. "He," she couldn't even say his name, "didn't kill you because he fell in love with you, Dani. He couldn't go through with it."

She remembered what he said at the hospital.

No matter what, I need you to know I love you. I have always loved you. That wasn't a lie. No matter what else may have been, that part wasn't.

"Remember?" she asked, and then repeated his words to Danielle.

"It's true. Nothing will ever absolve Clay of his sins. Nothing will ever give back what he took from you girls. Nothing will change what he did. But *he* changed. He truly loved you, Danielle. With all his heart. He didn't bring you here to isolate you from Gemma. He brought you here to protect you," Addie said.

Gemma couldn't take it anymore. Lots of questions remained, but one stuck out like the sorest of thumbs.

"Who are you?" she demanded of Addie. "How do you know all of this?"

"The doctor who discovered the *furia transformationem* antigen—"

"I didn't ask about him. I asked about *you*."

Dani put her hand on Gemma's knee, as if Gemma was the one who might transform into a Fury if not kept calm.

"I *was* that doctor's wife."

Gemma's head pounded. Sure, she'd been the one who'd asked. But she wasn't sure her brain could handle the response. She was on information overload. Each answer led to more questions.

"But you said the doctor's wife had an unfortunate encounter with a male Fury. That's what drove the doctor to begin—" Danielle began to voice Gemma's very thought, but Addie cut her off.

"I said she had an *unfortunate encounter*, yes," Addie said with a smile. "I didn't say he killed her. That man's name was Antoine. We had an affair. I fell deeply in love with him, but… as I said, my husband was a very, very wealthy man. I could've never left him. He would've taken our son and I never would've seen him again. Speaking of, excuse me for a moment won't you? I need to call my son."

Gemma and Dani exchanged a glance as Addie went out onto the porch.

A moment later, she returned and smoothly picked up her story where she'd stopped, as if she hadn't left, "When I told Antoine I couldn't leave my husband for him, he transformed. And he attacked me. He left me for dead. Like you, Dani, he didn't remember the transformation, or the attacks. He came to visit me in the hospital. When I told him what happened..." Addie looked down at her hands. "He couldn't handle it. He took his own life."

A tear rolled down Gemma's cheek. Dani reached up and wiped it away. Then Gemma did the same for Dani's tears.

"It haunted me, but for years... I believed my husband. The world was better off if Furies were destroyed as young as possible. It's unforgiveable. But one day I woke up and... I realized how wrong I was. He was. I vowed from that moment on, to never, ever let the same thing happen to anyone in the same... predicament. As I said, Danielle, you have the ability to become a Fury. But that's not who you are. You're a human being. My Antoine was a human being."

Gemma leaned forward, interested now. "So... you did leave your husband. But you're obviously still in contact with your son."

"Let's just say my husband... my late husband also had an unfortunate encounter where he was attacked. He didn't survive. His attacker was never found," Addie said. There was a self-satisfied gleam in her eye.

She killed him.

"Vengeance isn't always a bad thing. All those innocent children my husband had a hand in murdering. They deserved retribution, don't you think?" She gave a casual shrug. "I inherited everything my husband had, including the payout from his exorbitant life insurance policy."

"And you shut down his lab," Gemma said. "The testing, the treatments…"

"I did," Addie beamed with pride. "But he had devoted employees. Employees hellbent on fulfilling his life's mission. After I shut down the lab and the testing and the treatments, they formed the organization that Clay and, I suppose Agent Palmer, worked for. They operate so clandestinely; we haven't been able to find or shut them down. They have the master list of everyone with the gene, I'm afraid. And those that are still living, well, the organization exists for the sole purpose of finding them. But we have been able to keep them safe."

Until now, Gemma thought, and suspected Dani and Addie were thinking the exact same thing.

She also wondered exactly who the *we* Addie spoke of were and *how* they were able to keep the Furies safe.

Dani sat beside her, and Gemma could tell from her breathing she was being very intentional about each exhale, each inhale. Trying to keep herself from losing it.

"How do you know so much about Clay?" Dani asked Addie, looking betrayed.

There were so many other questions, Gemma tried not to get frustrated at Dani for thinking that one was the most important.

How did Addie know about their parents? How did Addie know about Gemma and Danielle? And what the hell was up with Harmony Springs? Yes, Clay was the one that convinced Danielle to move here… but their parents had bought the house here long before Clay ever came into the picture. And they'd left it to Dani in their will.

They wanted her to be here, Gemma thought. She'd always

known her parents had their reasons… but now she was starting to get an inkling of what those reasons might be.

Addie looked at Danielle, then Gemma, fondly. "There are many questions, loves. And many more answers, but—"

There was a soft knock at the door.

"Who could that be?" Gemma whispered. If it was another neighbor, one who'd already heard the news of Clay's demise and was dropping by with condolences and a casserole, Gemma would lose her mind.

Danielle grabbed Gemma's arm, moving closer to her, as if ready to hide behind her big sister for protection, the way she'd done when they were young. Gemma looked at her with a comforting glance, one she hoped said, *I'm here. I've got you. It'll be alright.*

Addie opened her mouth but was interrupted by a second knock, just as polite as the first.

"It's Sheriff Dobbs. Open up, please."

Of course, in Harmony Springs, even the cop would be courteous, lightly rapping on the door with their knuckles and waiting instead of banging for half a second before kicking it in.

"Shit," Danielle hissed. "He thinks Gemma killed Clay! Once he sees Palmer, he'll arrest her for sure!"

"Just a moment!" Addie called out. "Now, now, darling," she said to Danielle. "Let's remember the importance of keeping our wits about us."

Which was a fancy way of saying *Calm down.* And how often did that work?

Please do not choose this moment to transform, Dani.

"It's okay, Dani. If he does arrest me, call Randy Silverman," Gemma said, as soothingly as possible. But when she turned her attention to Addie, her tone was accusatory. "You lied to us when you told us you were calling your son, didn't you? You called the Sheriff instead."

"What?" Dani questioned, once again sounding betrayed. "I thought you were on our side, Addie."

"Don't doubt for a moment that I am. I didn't lie to you," Addie rose from her seat and strode towards the door. "I did call my son. My son *is* Sheriff Dobbs."

CHAPTER 15

"COME IN, ALBIE, COME IN," ADDIE GESTURED SHERIFF Dobbs inside.

"Mind blown," Gemma mouthed to Danielle, who nodded.

Was it possible in this scenario, the cop was one of the good guys?

"Ladies." Sheriff Dobbs tipped the brim of his hat at Gemma and Danielle. "Remain seated, please."

He glanced at Addie—his mother.

Mind blown indeed.

"In the kitchen," Addie told him. "Follow me."

He obeyed.

"I think Sheriff Dobbs is a mama's boy," Gemma whispered as they left the room. She playfully nudged Dani, trying to keep the mood light. Well, as light as a mood could be on a night like this. A *let's not transform into a Fury at least* level of light.

"What if Clay told Palmer where I was so Palmer could come and kill me?" Dani whispered. Gemma had never heard anyone sound so sad.

From the kitchen, Sheriff Dobbs let out a whistle. "What the hell happened in here?"

"You *know* what happened, Albert. Now get your boys in here and take care of it."

Gemma and Danielle exchanged a glance out of the corner of their eyes.

Gemma tried to follow Danielle's line of thinking. *Palmer killed Clay, made it look like a wild cat attack so he wouldn't be found out, but Dani Furied out and chased him off. So he went to the hospital, stabbed Clay, planned to frame that on Gemma and...* She hit the same snag she'd hit before. If killing Dani had been a part of the plan, why hadn't Palmer just killed her as soon as he broke in, then stashed the knife in the drawer, and framed both murders on Gemma?

Addie strode back in.

Wiping her hands together like she was brushing off dust, she offered a slight smile. "Albie's got a cleaning crew that will get things spick-and-span in there by sunup. It may take a few days to get things good as new, but we'll have the windows boarded up until we can get the panes replaced."

Sheriff Dobbs stepped back into the living room. "Just a few questions—"

Addie clapped her hands together. "No more questions, Albert!"

"Mother," Sheriff Dobbs said in a warning tone. These two obviously both thought they were the top dog. "This is a crime scene and I am the Sheriff. The crossbow." He shot a look at Gemma. "That belong to you, Ms. Jaeger, I assume? The arrows your handiwork?"

"Yes, Sheriff," Gemma said, watching her tone. "I acted in self-defense. The man broke into my sister's house. He planted a knife in one of the drawers in the kitchen. I suspect you'll find it's the same knife that killed my sister's husband."

The sheriff lifted his chin in acknowledgement. "Other

than the crossbow, either of you have any other weapons on the premises?"

There was no point in lying.

He may very well have a search warrant.

"Yeah," Gemma said. "They're all in the back bedroom."

"I'm going to need to confiscate those for the time being," Sheriff Dobbs said. Probably just wanting to throw his weight around.

Gemma flicked her gaze in Addie's direction, waiting to see if the older woman would intervene. She didn't.

"Obviously you ladies can't stay here tonight," he said.

"They'll both stay with me," Addie proclaimed.

Gemma watched as mother and son stared each other down in a battle of wills.

"Absolutely not," Sheriff Dobbs said. With a pointed look at Danielle, he added, "I'm not at all comfortable with that."

"She was provoked, Albert!"

"I'll get them a motel room over in Sevierville." he said to Addie, then to Gemma, "It's about twenty miles due north of here. It's not the nicest, but I know the owner and there'll be a vacancy."

"I thought Gemma couldn't leave town?" Dani asked, her voice quiet. Shame crept in at the edges.

"We'll make an exception in this case, ma'am. Why don't you go pack a bag, Mrs. Hickman? Miss Jaeger, come with me. Mother, go home. I've got it from here."

He started down the hall without waiting for a response from any of them.

Addie turned to Danielle. "Your sister was never a suspect, darling. Albie was instructed to tell her not to leave town because we didn't want her convincing you to leave."

"I belong here, don't I?" Dani asked. It broke Gemma's

heart that Dani sounded like she believed it. And it doubly broke Gemma's heart that she was starting to believe it, too.

"Everything is going to be okay, love. You'll see. You'll both have breakfast at my house in the morning. Eight o'clock. We still have quite a bit of talking to do. And no matter what, remember: Clay loved you. He truly did."

Without waiting for a response—*that must be a family trait*, Gemma thought—Addie exited through the front door, which Sheriff Dobbs had left ajar.

Dani looked at Gemma with red-rimmed eyes, filled with tears and panic.

"It'll be okay." Gemma squeezed Dani's knee, and as she did, she remembered the first sentence of gibberish Clay had said to her as they were wheeling him out of the room.

Gemma, I need you to PASS this WORD on.

PASS this WORD.

PASSWORD.

"Holy shit," Gemma whispered.

"Miss Jaeger, the night's not getting any younger!"

"Coming!" she called back to Dobbs. Then in an urgent whisper, she told Dani, "Sneak into the home office. Get Clay's laptop. Put it in your suitcase underneath your clothes so Dobbs doesn't know we have it."

Without question, Dani nodded.

A LITTLE OVER AN HOUR LATER, they were settled into the motel room Sheriff Dobbs had booked for them in Sevierville. The room was illuminated by a single lightbulb, suspended from the ceiling by a thin wire. The light was harsh and showed everything in sharp relief. All the furniture had seen better days. The king-sized bed had a lumpy mattress covered by a faded quilt. The dresser was missing one of its knobs, and the nightstand had a large water stain. The carpet was stained and threadbare in places. The windows were covered with heavy curtains that blocked out all the light.

But it was blood-free and quiet—and not in Harmony Springs—so it was good enough for Gemma. She was glad to be out of there, even if though it was only a temporary reprieve.

She thoroughly checked over the room as soon as they entered, looking under the bed, in the closets, behind the shower curtain. Until they found out more about this organization hellbent on wiping out Furies and Addie's plan for keeping Furies safe, Gemma wasn't taking any chances.

Now as Dani brushed her teeth and changed into PJs in the small bathroom, Gemma perched on the end of the bed, waiting. The sedative Dani had taken—along with the toll of the past few days—was starting to make her movements slower and her eyelids heavy. Her body was ready for sleep, even if her mind wasn't yet.

"All yours," Dani said, coming out and padding across the room to the bed. "You know, I completely understand if you don't feel comfortable sleeping in the same room with me, let alone the same bed. If you want to see if they have another free room now that we know what we know—"

"Absolutely not," Gemma said.

"Thank you," Dani whispered.

"Hey." Gemma stood and pulled her baby sister into her arms, into a fierce hug. Only when she squeezed Dani hard, did she wince. They both did. The adrenaline had worn off and now their bodies were feeling every bump, every bruise, every strained muscle.

"Not so tight please," Dani gritted through her teeth.

"Sorry," Gemma loosened her grip. She couldn't imagine how physically taxing shifting to Fury form and back had been on Dani.

"But you listen to me. You do not have to thank me for being here for you. Ever."

"I love you, Gemmie," Dani said, as they broke apart. They both wiped at their eyes. "There seems to be a couple of leaks in this room."

"You'll never get too old for me to tuck you in, you know," Gemma said, and then she did just that, kissing Dani on the forehead the way their mother used to do.

By the time Gemma finished getting ready for bed, Dani was already softly snoring.

Gemma turned off the overhead lights. Using the flashlight from her cell phone and careful not to make any noise, she unzipped Dani's suitcase and unearthed Clay's laptop. On the nightstand next to the bed was a cheap notepad with the motel chain's logo and a similarly branded pen. Gemma grabbed those, too. Taking everything to the wobbly table in front of the window, she set it down and booted it up. Then she sank into one of the chairs—also wobbly and with a loud creak.

She glanced over at the bed. In the faint glow from the computer's screen, she didn't see any movement, nor did she hear any signs that she'd woken her sister.

Closing her eyes, she pushed all other thoughts away from her mind. She focused on correctly recalling every single syllable Clay had said to her.

I will never forget our first HALLOWEEN together. I will ASK THE RISK. JAMES BOND is my favorite. I love your sister BACKWARDS and FORWARDS.

She was almost positive the password to Clay's

computer was hidden in plain sight within his words, which hadn't been gibberish at all.

She wrote *1031* down on the pad to represent Halloween.

ASK THE RISK was obviously asterisk.

James Bond was 007

And he loved her sister backwards and forwards.

inaddani, she wrote. She wondered if she should capitalize any of the letters and scratched it out, writing down *inaDDani* instead.

She held her breath as she typed 1031*007inaDDani in the password field and hit enter. She doubted she'd cracked the code on her first guess, but—

Instead of seeing the maddening *Password is incorrect. Try again.* message, the word *Welcome* appeared, with the spinning "I'm working" circle next to it.

Gemma gasped.

She was looking at Clay's desktop. The wallpaper was a picture of him and Dani, but it was like a jigsaw puzzle with many missing pieces so much of it was obscured by the many, many, many folders and shortcuts.

Gemma tried not to be frustrated. She thought she'd done the hardest part, but...

The fact that Clay had wanted her to have his password meant that there was something on his laptop he felt she and Dani needed to find.

But with the state of his desktop...

"Digital needle in a virtual haystack," she muttered under her breath.

Either Clay had been a very disorganized man, or this mess was intended to make certain materials hard to locate, unless you were the person who knew where you'd put them.

She had no idea what she was even looking for.

She opened up his list of recent documents.

Scanning the list, she groaned.

Document1

Document17

Document8

Document263

She clicked on the Documents folder, hoping the small sample wasn't an accurate representation of his overall labeling system.

But it was.

All the files were from a word processing program.

Clay was dead. Yet, he was still doing stuff to make her hate him more.

The scrolling seemed endless, until finally she got to Document99999.

Certainly there could not actually be 99999 documents. But perusing the list of chronological numbers, she didn't notice any missing. But her eyes glazed over, so she wouldn't bet any money on her accuracy. Who had that many documents? And how did Clay keep up with what any of them were?

She opened Document1.

And blinked.

Document2.

And blinked.

Both were blank.

Going back to the list, she scrolled again, this time paying attention to the file size. They were all between 12KB—the size of the two blanks—and 40KB.

She opened a couple of the files on the bigger end.

Dkladjklajdlkuoipuouiakl;l;12839u70987a had been copied and pasted over and over.

If this was a puzzle, she sure as hell didn't have time to solve it.

186

Turning to his browser, she tried to open Clay's email, but no luck there. His password wasn't saved. On the off chance he was one of those use-the-same-password-everywhere kind of people, which she seriously doubted, she tried the password for his laptop. No dice.

Next, she went to his pictures. Every single one was from his and Danielle's wedding day.

"Wait," she whispered.

His documents went up to 999999. The same number of digits used for a date in numerical form.

That's it.

She didn't know what she was about to uncover, but she knew it was *something*. With shaky fingers she raced to Document03132019. The date Clay and Dani had gotten married. Though it was one of the worst days of Gemma's life, if Clay had truly loved her sister, he would have considered it one of the best of his.

She opened it.

My Dearest Danielle, the first line read.

Gemma's heart sank.

She'd done all that work to discover a love letter to Dani?

Well.

Maybe at least it would give her sister some peace, some answers. Tangible proof that despite what he had done, Clay *had* loved her.

Gemma went to close out of the screen—this was private. For Dani.

Yet, before she could click the X, the next line caught her eye.

If something happens to me, I need you to follow these instructions very carefully.

Hooked, Gemma read on.

We get a quarterly stipend from the town of Harmony Springs.

"What?" Gemma whispered. That explained where the payments Clay got every three months came from, but it didn't explain *why*.

I transfer 3/4s of every stipend to an offshore account belonging to Sheriff Dobbs to ensure our safety. Keep making the payments. Do not tell anyone about this arrangement. And whatever you do, don't trust him. Don't trust anything he says. But stay in Harmony Springs. No trouble will find you here, as long as you do what I'm telling you.

Gemma read that line over and over again, trying to make sense of it. Wasn't that literally Dobbs' job, to keep the residents of Harmony Springs—of which Dani was one—safe?

She pinched the bridge of her nose, trying to ease her pounding head so she could *think*.

"Dobbs was extorting Clay," Gemma whispered.

That was the only explanation, but it only led to more questions.

It may have answered an outstanding question, though.

"Oh, dear," Addie had said. *"They've found us. How is it possible?"*

I have a feeling your precious son Albie might know, Addie, Gemma thought.

She re-read the message Clay had written in the document again.

Had Clay been paying the Sheriff not tell the organization he'd formerly worked for his whereabouts?

"It makes so much sense," Gemma said, out loud.

She glanced over to make sure she hadn't woken Dani. There was no movement in the bed. But... the heavy curtains covering the windows... was Gemma hallucinating because she was so bone tired... or had they swayed ever-so-slightly?

CHAPTER 16

Fᴜᴄᴋ ɪᴛ ᴀʟʟ, ꜱʜᴇ ʜᴀᴅ ᴄʜᴇᴄᴋᴇᴅ ᴇᴠᴇʀʏᴡʜᴇʀᴇ *EXCEPT* behind the curtains.

Gemma's heart sped up. The racing pulse was her gut telling her something was wrong. She wasn't being paranoid. Her body didn't do irrational fear.

She squinted down at the floor, where the hem of the curtain brushed the ancient carpet. She half-expected to see the toes of a man's loafers sticking out.

"Damn, it's late," she said to herself, fiddling with her phone, which was laying on the table next to the laptop. Her yawn started out fake but turned real. "Half an hour power nap, and then I'm back to it."

Gemma stood. Listening carefully, she took one step at a time towards the bed, ready to fight in case someone lunged from behind the curtains and grabbed her from behind. No one did.

But still, she was positive someone else was in the room.

Sheriff Dobbs is in the room.

He'd set the trap and she'd brought Dani right into it.

But why?

She inched closer to the bed.

Then.

There. There it was.

A soft chuckle.

"Too easy," he whispered.

She heard his footsteps closing in.

"I'm going to need you to freeze, little lady," he said. "Put those hands up and turn around slowly."

Fuck.

She did as he said and found herself staring at the business end of his revolver.

She didn't flinch, didn't show one iota of weakness.

"I want to look into those pretty brown eyes when I put a bullet through your forehead," Dobbs said.

But Gemma knew she still had an advantage here. If he'd merely wanted her dead, he would've shot her already. He wanted to play a little first. That was fine. She could play.

The thing about a human male who'd gotten away with something… they were rarely content to get away with it. They were driven by the irrepressible need to brag about the amazing feat they'd pulled off.

She and Sheriff Dobbs likely had very different plans for the outcome of this stand-off. He wasn't going to win, but she might as well get all the information she could out of him while he thought his victory was certain.

"Shame I got all your weapons," he said. "This is hardly a fair fight."

Fair.

Gemma rolled her eyes.

This man wouldn't know fair if it came up, introduced itself, and bit his penis off.

"So it's you that's been following me," Gemma said, lifting her chin.

"Well, technically, I didn't follow you to this dump," he gestured around the room with his gun, his eyes following it in every direction he pointed. She could've kicked it right out of his hand in that one second of distraction, but she really didn't want to have to wrestle him for it. "Since I took a little shortcut and got here first, but yeah, from the moment you drove that little Jeep of yours into Harmony Springs, babe. Once we found out that your sister called for you to come to her… Well. You fucked up our plan."

"And when you say our, you mean you and Agent Palmer?" Gemma asked.

Dobbs laughed, low and cruel. "So the little lady wants one more bedtime story before she takes the big sleep?"

If you call me little lady one more time…

"Alright. I'll humor you. Yep. Me and Palmer. To be honest, you and I wouldn't be standing here having this little talk if Palmer wasn't incompetent. If he had taken out Clay that night like he was supposed to instead of running like a girl," Dobbs shook his head. "Fucking idiot."

Yeah, you really are.

"So… Palmer was supposed to kill Clay, and then what?"

"Your sister would take off, leaving a note behind that it was too painful to stay in Harmony Springs with Clay gone." He smirked. "Or, at least, that's what my bleeding-heart mother would think."

"I'm going to need you to back up a bit, because I still don't understand," Gemma said as sweetly as possible. "I know Clay was paying you off. To keep Palmer from finding him?"

"Hell no. That was hush money but had nothing to do with Palmer. When I made that l'il deal with your BIL, I didn't even know who Palmer was."

Gemma couldn't decide if she was more exhausted or confused, but she had to push both aside. Once this conversation came to an end, it was going to be a literal fight to the death. Unless Dani wanted to wake up and Fury out and take care of Dobbs.

"Hickman was paying me not to tell your sister all his deep dark secrets. Y'know, how he offed your mommy and daddy and whatnot."

Gemma's hands clenched into fists. Adrenaline coursed through her body, clearing her head, and waking her up.

"How did you know his deep dark secrets?" Gemma asked. "I can't imagine the two of you went out for a couple of drinks and he just spilled his guts."

"No, he didn't spill his guts to *me*," Dobbs laughed, though Gemma couldn't figure out what the hell was funny. "Anyway," Dobbs went on. "The night Clay was supposed to kill your sister… He wouldn't have even had the balls to attack her if he hadn't needed proof of death. He sent it to his boss, who fell for it. I mean, he didn't look into it any further? He didn't, like, check for an obit? Just saw the picture and was like, yeah, okay, she looks dead, she must be dead."

Gemma waited.

"But he wised up when Clay just seemed to vanish off the face of the planet. Realized something was fishy. Then he did some digging. Of course, by then, Clay'd married your sister, whisked her to Harmony Springs, where they were the Smiths. He thought he was so clever, thinking they'd live happily ever after here." Dobbs nodded. "And they might have, too, if I hadn't come across a post his boss made a few months back on a Fury board on the dark web. Looking for a Clay Hickman. Who looked an awful lot like Harmony Springs' very own Clay Smith."

Everything started to gel in Gemma's brain. "The boss was Palmer."

She'd had it backwards. Clay had worked for Palmer, not the other way around.

"Ding, ding, ding!" Dobbs crowed.

"And I'm assuming you reached out to find out what kind of deal he'd offer you?"

"I did, I did. And his offer was much better than the paltry sum I was squeezing out of your sister's doting hubby." He shook his head as if he couldn't believe his own genius. "Get this. We were going to take the Furies one by one. It would be a slow process so no one in Harmony Springs would get suspicious. But we'd get one, leave a note saying she'd decided to leave Harmony Springs for whatever reason, and no one would be the wiser. Each payday when we turned in their bodies would be so frickin' enormous even split between me and Palmer. It seemed fair. I'd pick the best marks, and he'd take them out and hand them over to his supervisor at the organization. Mom would be none the wiser and keep bringing us fresh meat, so there would be an endless supply. So when ol' Sam Powell died a very unfortunate death and, wow, what luck, a position opened up in Harmony Springs, I brought in Palmer to fill it."

"You killed Powell," Gemma said.

Dobbs shrugged.

Whether he realized it or not, his and Palmer's plan had a whole bunch of holes in it, but Gemma knew when to keep quiet. There was no point in showing him the flaws in his thinking.

But… was he saying Harmony Springs was basically full of Furies?

"Of course, you showing up here made things more complicated than they needed to be. But, hey, I don't have to cut Palmer in anymore, so I guess I should thank you for that."

"Let me guess," Gemma said. "You arranged for the attack on Clay to look like a wild cat did it so if anyone found out otherwise, you could blame it all on Palmer, since he was investigating?"

"You are such a smart girl. It's too bad you have to die. Gotta keep my hands clean. It would break Mom's heart if she knew the truth. Fortunately… she never will."

I wouldn't be so sure about that.

"So," Gemma began, because shutting down Palmer and Dobbs wasn't enough. She needed to make sure that communication between anyone and everyone that would lead the organization to Dani was thoroughly severed. "What's your plan now?"

"Kill you, obviously. Kill your sister. Hand her over to the organization. Tell Mom Danielle said she couldn't handle being in Harmony Springs with her dearest hubby dead, so she went back to Bumfuck, Wherever with you."

Gemma shook her head. "She won't believe you. She cared about Dani too much. She'll come looking for her."

"And when she doesn't find her—or you—she'll decide that you were too scared to go back where you could be found, so you both went into hiding. It's a foolproof plan," he smirked, his voice bloated with ego.

Oh, God, I hope not, Gemma thought.

"Well, I killed your contact with the organization. Yeah, you don't have to cut him in anymore, but you don't have anyone to do his part of the job, anymore, either. So… how you gonna turn her over? Google clandestine fury organization?"

"I got two things off Palmer while I was in your sister's kitchen checking things out. His phone, which I'm sure has his supervisor's number on it… and his finger, which will unlock it for me."

Thinking of the implications of his last statement, bile rose in Gemma's throat.

"Okay. Enough chit-chat," Dobbs said.

"I agree," Gemma nodded. "One last question, though…"

"All right. Shoot."

Now Gemma smirked. While they'd been talking, she'd lowered her hands so gradually, Dobbs—enraptured the tale he spun of his own sheer brilliance—hadn't even noticed.

"You got Palmer's phone and his finger. But what about his gun?" she asked, knowing he didn't have it… because she did. She'd had her hands in the deep pockets of her pajamas for a few minutes now, her fingers on Palmer's pistol. She'd slipped into the kitchen and taken it before joining Dobbs for him to confiscate her weapons.

"He didn't have a gun on him," Dobbs said, still not realizing that though she may have walked into his trap initially… now she'd lured him into hers. He didn't sound sure. He'd been so busy thinking about the phone and the finger and keeping his honeypot, he hadn't checked.

"Oh, yeah, he did, actually," Gemma said. She'd whipped it out, aimed, and fired off a round before he even registered what was happening.

She hoped the silencer Palmer had generously provided her with would ensure that the gunshots wouldn't wake the entire motel. As it turned out, they didn't even wake up Dani.

Dobbs swayed back and forth. Then he staggered backwards. Then he lunged at Gemma before falling like a tree with shallow roots in a Category Five Hurricane.

When he hit the floor with a thud, Dani moaned, "Gemma, what the hell? I'm trying to sleep."

After checking a few things—like to make sure Dobbs didn't have a pulse, Gemma went over and shook her sister.

"Dani, I'm going to need you to wake up. And not freak out."

CHAPTER 17

DANI HAD FREAKED OUT. "OH, MY GOD! WHAT ARE WE going to do!"

"Well, we're going to inform the next of kin," Gemma said.

"We cannot tell Ms. Coffey you killed her son! Oh, my God, Gemma, you killed her son! She is never going to believe you had a good reason for it! She's never going to believe it was self-defense."

Dani was pacing back and forth, raking her hands through her hair, and it was making Gemma very nervous.

"She will believe us, Dani," Gemma said. "Because he's going to confess to everything he did."

Dani blinked at her incredulously, as if she'd just sprouted a horn.

She nudged Dobb's hand with her socked foot and then leapt back as if she was afraid he was going to spring to life and grab her ankle. "Um… dead men tend to not confess, Gemmie."

"Everything's recorded on my phone," Gemma said. "I already checked to make sure. You can hear it all, loud and clear."

Dani practically bum rushed her. Hugging Gemma

tight, she whispered, "My sister is the bravest, badassest, most brilliant woman on the planet."

"I don't think badassest is a word," Gemma said, with tears running down her cheeks. She wasn't sure if they were happy tears or sad tears, or some combination of both, but she was sure glad she had her sister's shoulder to cry on. And she would be the same for Dani. Hopefully for the rest of their lives.

THE NEXT MORNING, Gemma woke up in Adeline Coffey's guest room. When she'd gone to sleep, Dani's elbow had been in her side. But now the other side of the small bed was vacant.

The previous day—morning, afternoon, night, late night, middle of the night—all came rushing back to her, making her slightly dizzy, slightly nausea, and tremendously homesick. Not for East Haven. Not for the Moonlight Bar. But for Matt.

She picked up her phone.

"Hey, you." She could hear his smile when he answered on the first ring.

"Is it too early?" she asked.

He laughed. "It's almost noon."

"What?" she hadn't even glanced at the time on her phone or the bedside clock before calling. But both confirmed he was correct. "Oh. Wow. Yesterday felt like about three weeks, so… I guess my body needed the rest."

"Well, I'm glad you got it," he said.

"I think you should quit the paper and start your own business," she blurted. "Maybe like… an online news outlet where you can tell the stories you want to tell."

It was messed up, she knew. A man who wanted

nothing more than to expose the truth dating a woman who had to actively work to keep it hidden. But…

Uh-oh. Did my mind just go there? Did I just mentally acknowledge that Matt and I are dating?

"Where is this coming from?" Matt asked.

"Um. I don't know," she admitted. "Life's too short. I want you to be happy."

"Well, it's definitely something to think about, though, you know, I do have bills to pay. Being an adult sucks sometimes."

"You can say that again," she agreed.

"Speaking of adult things that suck… Is there anything I can do to help with the arrangements for Clay's funeral?"

"We haven't even talked about that yet," Gemma said. "But I appreciate your offering."

"Okay. I don't want to nag, but any idea when I might see that gorgeous face of yours?"

She started to suggest switching to a video call but then remembered the last time she'd caught sight of her reflection, she had a nasty bruise on her right cheek and the beginnings of a black eye. So some concealer would definitely be in order before he saw her face.

"I'll be back as soon as I can," she said. "I miss you."

There was a moment of stunned silence.

"I miss you, too," he said. Once again, she could hear his smile.

Wrapping up the call, she got up, stretched, and wandered down the hall. Every bone in her body screamed with every step.

She could hear Dani and Addie's voices drifting in from the kitchen.

"I don't know what hurts more. Losing him or losing who I believed him to be, as well. The thing is, I should hate him, right? But... I can't reconcile what he did with the man I believed he was."

That was Addie, speaking about Sheriff Dobbs. Her son. Her Albie.

"I know exactly what you mean," Dani said.

"I know you do, love. I'm saddened that either of us have to go through this, but glad we have each other to go through it with."

There would have been a time where those words would've set Gemma ablaze with jealousy. But now she knew, she couldn't possibly fathom what Dani was feeling. Ms. Coffey—Addie—could.

She was the one Danielle needed to see her through this.

But that didn't mean Gemma was going to walk—or be pushed—out of Dani's life again. That would never, ever happen.

But there were still unanswered questions and before Gemma would even consider going back to East Haven and leaving Dani here... she was going to need to know everything about Harmony Springs.

She cleared her throat, so Dani and Addie were aware of her presence before she barged in.

This morning, Addie looked strong and put together. The night before, when she'd arrived at the motel, she'd collapsed on her knees next to Sheriff Dobbs' lifeless body. Her body had convulsed with grief. Dani had held her while she'd sobbed.

But Addie had listened to the recording with a quiet acceptance and grace Gemma couldn't fathom. Afterwards, she'd listened to Gemma's explanation of everything she'd learned that had led to the conversation that took place between herself and Dobbs. Then Addie had calmly called Sheriff Dobbs' team to come clean up yet another crime scene. She gathered up Dani and Gemma and brought them back here.

"Come in, dearheart," Addie beckoned to Gemma as soon as she stepped into the doorway between the kitchen and the hall. "Join us."

Gemma padded in and sat at the table.

"Are you hungry? Thirsty?" Addie asked.

Gemma shook her head. "I know that yesterday was one of the worst days of your life, Addie. And yours, too, Dani. But Addie, I need to know everything about Harmony Springs. It's obviously not your normal town."

"That it isn't." Addie agreed. Despite everything, a smile played about her lips.

"Wait," Dani interrupted. "First. How did you know about me? How did you know our parents? How did you know so much about Clay?"

"We're going to need some sweets to get through all those questions," Addie said.

A few minutes later, there was a spread of cookies, brownies, and doughnuts before them. They each had a cup of coffee. Addie took a sip from her mug and a bite of a chocolate chip cookie.

"I told you that my former husband's former employees had the master list of children with *furia transformationem* gene. But so did I. I reached out to all the parents who'd declined the treatment for their kids, offering an alternative solution."

"What was this alternative solution?" Gemma asked.

"The option to purchase a home in Harmony Springs for a very reasonable price."

Gemma and Dani exchanged glances. She could practically see the lightbulb come on behind Dani's eyes at the same time she put two and two together.

"All that money you got from your husband, from his life insurance policy…" Gemma said.

"You used it to buy Harmony Springs," Dani finished.

They smiled shyly at each other. It had been a long time since one of them finished the other's sentence.

"Clever young ladies, both of you. I used it to *build* Harmony Springs," Addie nodded. "It was just land when I bought it, but… there was something about this place. About the Springs themselves. The weather that's always perfect, the flowers that bloom year round. Let's say I saw the magic that already existed here and cultivated it, for children like you, Danielle. So you could grow up into an adult and live your life. The environment is carefully controlled to suppress all of your Fury instincts. There are no triggers. We make sure of it."

Gemma didn't feel the need to bring it up, but she briefly wondered if Clay had ever been under a medically induced coma at all. Perhaps he'd slipped into the coma after Palmer attacked him and the medical staff legitimately hadn't known if he would regain consciousness, but they'd told Dani the alternate, less upsetting story.

"There's only tranquility," Addie went on. "Peace and quiet. Every resident of Harmony Springs is either a family with a member who has the *furia transformationem* gene or one of my team. It is our duty to help take care of those who might shift and those who have shifted but wish to live in peace. Dani, that's part of why I suggest you take daily swims in the Springs. When you do, it soothes your soul. When I take a dip in the Springs, I look like this instead of my inner ancient old crone." She laughed. "But seriously. Everything here is designed to give you the life you deserve."

"Wait. When Clay moved Dani here…" Gemma began.

"When Clay and I moved here," Dani corrected. "You can't blame everything on him, Gemmie. I made some decisions on my own."

"When Clay and Dani moved here," Gemma said. "Did Clay know what Harmony Springs was?"

Addie shook her head. "He had no idea. He only wanted to move Dani from East Haven, to get her somewhere safe. He believed in order to do that, it was necessary to sever all ties with the past. When she mentioned having the house here, it seemed the perfect solution." Her eyes filled with tears. "I'm only sorry that Albie... He betrayed you. He betrayed me. He betrayed all of us."

Gemma closed her eyes, processing. That's why Clay had convinced Dani to cut her off? To keep her safe?

Dani put her hand over Addie's. "That's not your fault, Addie. Please don't blame yourself. You had no idea."

Addie wiped a stray tear from the corner of her eye.

"I can't believe our parents never told us any of this," Gemma said. She'd been sitting quietly, listening, processing.

"I believe they intended to when it became necessary. But they never imagined they'd leave you both so soon."

"I have a question," Dani's voice was so timid.

"What is it, love?" Addie asked.

"Why didn't I transform when Clay," she paused and swallowed hard. "When he came to kill Mom and Dad? I could've saved them."

"No," Gemma said. "You can't control it. You cannot blame yourself for—"

"I should've felt the vengeance after seeing them shot, Gemma! I should've—"

"You were too young," Addie interrupted. "My former husband—or evil ex, whichever you prefer—found strong proof that no one with the gene shifted until they were 25 years of age. That's why he accepted it when the parents said no to the treatment. He didn't like it, mind you, but he knew there would be time to intervene in other ways later. I suspect that he'd already laid the groundwork for the kill organization. Speaking of, we no longer have to worry about that. I used Palmer's finger to unlock his phone myself. His only contact was a woman named Irene."

So he did have a wife? Gemma thought. She'd been certain he was lying.

"It was clear from their messages she was his supervisor. She still thought he was in Vegas. Had no idea he'd relocated here. Anyway, I resigned on his behalf. Said he was retiring to Florida, so if they go looking for him..." she shrugged, blithely.

Gemma had no doubts that even if Irene tried to find out where the call had originated, she wouldn't ever be able to figure it out. She was sure, like with the wonky Wi-Fi and what was accessible via the internet and what was not, Addie had that covered.

"How do we know Palmer and Sheriff Dobbs—Albie —didn't tell anyone else about their scheme, though?" Dani asked, worriedly.

Gemma had had the same fear... until she really mulled it over.

"They were both greedy bastards," she said, then added, to Addie, "no offense. If they told anyone else where all the Furies they'd planned to turn in," Gemma shuddered, "were... They risked being cut out altogether. They'd become mere middlemen, indispensable. Why pay for someone to bring something to you, when you can just go get it yourself?"

Addie nodded. "You—and all of the others—are really and truly safe here. And I hope you'll stay. Your inner Fury will be kept pacified here, I promise you that.

I failed you once. I will not fail you again," Addie promised. "We're revisiting all our protocols. Ensuring that nothing will ever, ever slip through the cracks again."

Dani looked at Gemma. "That means I won't need you to take care of me," she said. "But I will always need you to be a part of my life. Split a sugar cookie with me?"

Gemma smiled. "I thought you'd never ask."

They ate their cookies and sipped their coffee.

Then, at the exact same moment, they asked, "How did you know so much about Clay?"

"You two are really something else, aren't you?" Addie clucked her tongue, but couldn't hide her grin. "Well, as Danielle knows, anyone moving into Harmony Springs is required to have counseling with Dr. Downs. Therapy is vital for those with the gene, of course, but for family members, as well. Among other things, Dr. Downs practices hypnotherapy. During a session, Clay confessed everything to her. What he did to your parents. What he did to you. The organization he worked for. The organization he left, to save you, to be with you."

Gemma felt her hackles going up. "And you just… I don't know… let it go?"

"We most certainly did not," Addie said. "But we did believe he'd truly changed. That he truly loved your sister and wanted what was best for her. We all felt it be best Danielle not know her true nature yet. She still hadn't completely healed from the trauma of losing your parents. And we agreed it was obviously best she not know about Clay's role in that. Their love was real. That's what we needed to focus on. That, and keeping Danielle safe, which was a common goal."

Gemma bit her lip. She wasn't sure how she felt about all of this. How she *should* feel about all of this. From the look on her sister's face, she could tell Dani was as equally conflicted.

"Albert had access to every building in the town. I suspect he was snooping regularly in Dr. Downs' office, reading her session transcripts and that's how he found out about Clay, in order to extort him of three-quarters of the stipend we pay to all family members, to cover their living expenses, which we try to keep to a minimum since bills are stressful," Addie said.

"There's no possibility Dr. Downs was involved?" Gemma asked.

"None," Addie said.

"I mean… it is a bit unethical to practice hypnotherapy on people without their knowledge, is it not?"

"Some might look at it that way, Gemma. But Dr. Downs and I looked at it as we have to protect those under our care, and their vulnerabilities from being exploited and exposed, at all costs."

Gemma glanced at Dani. How could she argue with that?

"But… Clay's consulting business wasn't actually making any money?" Gemma asked.

Addie shook her head. "The business was just a pretense. There aren't many opportunities for employment here because jobs aren't really needed. He went to that office all day every day and read, or watched television, under the pretense of going to work. He wanted to help us find the organization, but we couldn't risk him getting involved, being found. We couldn't have Dani worried about finances, nor could we explain to her why our town was essentially paying them to live here. Brynn —who is Dr. Downs' daughter—was there to closely monitor him."

"Clay was always very good with money," Dani said.

The wistful look in her eye saddened Gemma. "I can see how he could make ¼ of what we were getting work."

"So…" Addie asked. "Does that cover everything?"

"No," Gemma said. Now she had to ask the question she really wanted to ask. "I've heard a lot about it not being the right time. It not being the right time for Dani to have kids. It not being the right time for Dani to invite me to visit. About her waiting until she was ready. All of that was Dr. Downs, right? I mean, I know originally it was Clay's idea…but Dr. Downs agreed? That I'd be bad for Dani?"

Addie shook her head, then nodded. "Let me be clear. Dr. Downs never intended to keep you out of Dani's life permanently. It was always the intent to reunite you two. But Dani has a lot of repressed memories—which Dr. Downs will help you uncover, if and when you're ready, Dani—and she felt it necessary to not do anything that might bring those to the surface."

"Because it might cause my first shift," Dani said.

"Exactly," Addie said. "I know that doesn't make your time apart any easier… but does it at least help you understand it?"

Gemma looked at Dani. Dani nodded.

"I think so," Gemma said.

"Then I'm going to head over to your house to oversee the repairs," Addie said. "And to give you two some privacy."

After Addie left, Gemma and Dani were quiet for a moment.

Gemma picked up a brownie and broke it in two, passing the other half to Dani.

"You're staying, right?" Gemma asked. "In Harmony Springs?"

"I don't want to hurt anyone again," Dani said. "I

couldn't live with myself thinking I was a constant danger to everyone around me. I don't want to transform again. Ever." She nibbled on her brownie. "Will you be mad if I stay?"

Mad, no. Gemma felt a lot of emotions, but mad wasn't one of them.

"Not if I can come back and visit, like, all the time," she said.

"You'd better," Dani said. "I am so sorry for the time we lost, Gemmie."

Gemma stared fiercely into her sister's eyes, her heart full of love. "We will make up for every minute."

This time, Dani picked up a brownie, split it, and passed half to Gemma. They clinked brownies as if they were wine glasses. "Cheers to that."

Gemma went speechless, realizing that she'd made it through the past 24 hours without wanting a drink. Of course, she knew that didn't mean she was "cured". Just like with Dani's condition, hers would always remain inside of her, hopefully dormant, but always a breath away from being woken. She'd just been too damn busy to think about alcohol.

"On another note," Danielle said. "Are you going to tell Matt?"

"Excuse me?" Gemma asked.

"Are you going to tell him how you really feel about him?"

Gemma laughed. Not at the question, but because Matt was the first thing she thought of in the morning and the last thing at night. And she was finally, finally, ready to admit it.

"Because… listen…" Dani paused. "I know it's messed up, but… even knowing everything I know…" She took a deep breath, then huffed out an exhale. "I don't regret loving Clay. I don't regret being loved by Clay. Life's too short, Gemmie. If you love him, tell him. But more than that, if you love him… let yourself."

Life's too short. She'd said the same thing to Matt, when she'd proposed the wild idea of him quitting his job and starting his own business.

"To tell you the truth, I do think it's time," Gemma admitted.

"Really?" Dani raised her eyebrows at her sister over the rim of her mug.

"I think it's time to take our relationship to the next level."

"Hmm, that sounds very naughty."

Gemma grinned. No doubt parts of it would be. But it would finally be more than that. So much more.

"Maybe one day I'll learn how to control this," Danielle said, moving her hands across herself. "And I'll be able to come visit you—and Matt— back home in East Haven, too."

"I know you will. You can do anything."

"With my big sis beside me, I can for sure."

CHAPTER 18

GEMMA HAD BEEN IN HARMONY SPRINGS FOR A LITTLE over a week. Though it wasn't as creepy now that she understood it, it definitely was not home.

"You know, I'm finally thinking…" she said gently to Dani, after lunch. "It's time for me to go."

"I know," Danielle said. "I figured. That's why I got Chinese take-out again. I wanted to make sure you had some eggrolls to take with you. Snacks for the road."

Gemma smiled. "You know I'm not going to say no!"

"I want you to call me as soon as you get back to East Haven. Let me know you arrived safely."

"I will."

"You promise?"

"Of course," Gemma said. "And I'll be back before you know it."

They'd already discussed plans for her next visit.

"Have you decided what you're going to tell Matt… and what you're not?" Danielle asked.

"I guess I will have to tell him the truth. The whole truth."

"Do you think he will be able to handle it?"

"I hope that he can, because… I'm pretty sure I do love him."

"I'm pretty sure you do, too. And I am so happy for you, Gemma."

"I'm going to miss you."

"Same here."

Less than an hour later, Gemma was headed out to her Jeep. She knew her sister was going to be all right. Danielle had Addie and Dr. Downs and a whole community that would help her every single day. And Gemma was only a phone call away if Danielle ever needed her.

The drive to East Haven gave Gemma a renewed sense of purpose. She knew her family was important. A legacy. And she had been hiding from what she truly was. Whether she was actively hunting or not, she was a Hunter, just like her parents and their parents had been. It was part of who she was. It always would be. And it was time for her to embrace that.

SHE'D BEEN HOME for less than two hours when Matt knocked on her door with a hot croissant and a large Frappuccino with extra whipped cream.

"Come in," she said. "Let's go sit for a minute."

She wanted to hug him. To kiss him. To rip off all his clothes and make love to him. Then tell him that she was in love with him.

But his hands were full, for starters.

And they needed to talk first.

"How's your sister?"

"She's going to be fine," Gemma said. She sat down on the couch and patted the cushion next to hers. "Sit that stuff on the coffee table."

Matt glanced at her. The worry in his eyes was undeniable. "How are you?"

"I'm going to be fine, too," she said. Then it dawned on her. He should be at work right now. "Did you quit your job?"

"No. I'm playing hooky this afternoon to spoil you. I hope you don't mind."

"Mind?" she responded. "Why would I mind?"

"Come on, then. Eat before it gets cold—"

Gemma rose. "In a minute. I need to come clean with you about some things."

"Should I be worried?"

"Yes. I mean, not like that. It's just," she paused, looking for the right words. "Matt, there are things I realize I should have explained a long time ago, but I was hesitant about how you would react."

Matt's muscles tensed as he steadied himself. "Okay. Tell me."

"First of, I love you."

A big, broad grin spread across his face. Gemma felt the blush creeping up her neck as he leaned forward and kissed her on her forehead.

"That was something I already knew, Gems. I already felt it, even if you were scared to accept it. You just had to admit it to yourself."

"Well. I have officially admitted it to myself."

"Good. Because I love you, too."

"Before you commit to that... there's more. I have something I need to show you."

Gemma took his hand, pulling him and guiding him to her bedroom.

"I think I know what you're going to show me, and I've seen it quite a few times, but... I'm always happy to see it again," he teased.

She shook her head. "It's in here."

She let him into the walk-in closet.

Gemma pulled the old trunk forward. Retrieved the key. Unlocked it. The hinges squeaked as she lifted the lid.

Thankfully, Addie had retrieved all her weapons and returned them.

Gemma hadn't rewrapped them, so they were all laid bare, for Matt to see.

His eyes got big.

"Gems... what is all of this?"

"This," she said, at last letting down her walls, "is my story, Matt."

UNEARTH THE SECRETS, **face your fears, and dive into the heart-pounding supernatural mysteries of East Haven in Book 2!**

GEMMA'S RULE of staying out of the supernatural world shatters as a killer lurks in the shadows. With time ticking away and a sinister witch on the loose, Gemma's dark secret becomes her only weapon. Will she break her one rule and save innocent lives? Join her on this thrilling journey, but beware – danger lurks on every page.

CHAPTER 1

"Have I officially welcomed you back yet?" Drew, the bartender, asked as Gemma

settled onto her favorite stool. The happy hour rush buzzed around them.

Gemma closed her eyes for a second, listening to the sounds of the Moonlight Bar—her bar. When she looked back at the other woman, Gemma's lips slid into a small smile. "Once or twice."

"Well," Drew said, "third time's a charm. Welcome back, boss. The usual?"

"Yes, please."

"One Coke, coming up."

Despite everything she'd been through in the past few months, Gemma hadn't returned to drinking, and she was damn proud of herself for it.

Gemma glanced around.

The Moonlight Bar was more than her livelihood. It was her home. Some things had changed while she was away with her sister, but the peace this place brought her soul would never fade.

Never say never, she thought as a broad man with a gnarly ginger-colored beard caught her gaze and beckoned her over. She let out a little sigh, hesitating momentarily before standing and making her way to him, greeting regulars as she passed them.

Her bar was a haven for Hunters now. She loved that they were all welcome here. But that didn't mean she had to like them all.

"What can I do for you, Carson?" she asked the man who'd summoned her.

Carson Baker had only moved into the city a few months ago, so Gemma didn't know him well. Still, she did know that when this particular Hunter turned up at The Moonlight Bar, he wasn't seeking booze, camaraderie, or even the solace of being who he was—what he was—in plain sight.

No, Carson always brought an agenda in with him. And his agenda always conflicted with Gemma's ability to maintain a good mood.

Before responding, Carson took a long pull of his dark beer. Leaning back in his seat and crossing his arms over his chest, he leveled her with a reproving glare. Gemma steeled herself for Carson's latest update about their community's precarious state of affairs.

"Now more than ever, it's critical for every Hunter to have boots on the ground out there."

She kept her expression impassive. No matter how impassioned the plea he had at ready for her tonight, she would not be moved by it. She would refuse every call to action he issued, past, present, and future. Mirroring his resolute posture, she hoped her crossed arms put up a shield against his words and how right they were.

"Speaking of boots," she said, kicking his foot lightly with hers underneath the table. "Would you wipe some mud off yours before tracking it all over my floors? God, do you stomp in puddles like a child?"

This wasn't the first time she'd made this request, and she suspected it wouldn't be the last.

"My apologies. I forget. Have other things on my mind, y'know. And you know I'm right, Jaeger."

They both knew he was right, but she could not get involved.

For fuck's sake, her parents had been killed. And though she had survived, barely, her sister Danielle had been brutally attacked. Both traumatic events had been a direct consequence of the Hunter's life. Both traumatic results led to Gemma and Danielle's estrangement.

Gratitude washed over Gemma. But as thankful as she was that she and Danielle finally reconnected, some damage was irreparable. They'd never be as close as they once were.

Carson watched Gemma expectantly. When she didn't immediately respond, he added, "We're outnumbered."

But that was just stating the obvious.

"Hunters have always been outnumbered, Carson. Always will be." She lowered her voice, more out of habit than a necessity now. "As far as those proverbial boots," she paused to make air quotes around the word, "an extra pair on the ground won't make any difference. I hung mine up years ago. For good."

"Gemma." Her name came out of Carson's voice, wrapped in a blanket of urgency. "People are getting hurt. People are dying. Innocent people, people who—"

Gemma cut him off with a quick, slight shrug, and that's all she had to give.

No.

She'd give the Hunters shelter and a place to drink away their sorrows. *That* was all she had to offer. And it would have to be enough.

My hunting days are over, she thought. *I won't have any more blood on my hands.*

"There was another killing not far from here. Did you know that?" Carson asked, presenting the question in a sinister tone to drive fear into her. His eyes flashed, and he continued ominously, "Soon, the danger will be at your back door. Then what?"

He sounded like one of those late-night public service announcements that ran on television in a bygone era. *Do you know where your children are?*

But, again, she had to acknowledge that he was right. The paranormal battle raged around them whether she chose to step onto the battlefield or not. Once you were aware of that battle, you could never forget it. But she refused to let his warnings reignite any embers of fight that still smoldered deep inside her soul.

She clenched her jaw.

Why couldn't she finally enjoy the quiet and, yes, peaceful life she'd worked so hard to build for herself? Was the desire to do so selfish, all things considered? Yes. Maybe. But she'd spent so long in her self-made cocoon of self-destruction and isolation, never allowing herself the luxury of caring about anyone or anything. Then Matt had come along. It had taken him so long, but he'd made a place for himself in her heart. She'd let down her walls long enough to let him in.

And she was terrified of losing him.

Carson lifted one eyebrow. "So, you really gonna wait until you don't have a choice, Gemma?"

She bristled but didn't give him the satisfaction of seeing her squirm. Even though she didn't owe him an explanation for her decision, Gemma gestured around them and said, "Look. This bar is my concern now. This is my life now."

"Hey, I know I'm beating a dead horse," he said, his hands raised in surrender. "But I gotta keep beating it. Hopefully, it'll come back to life one day, eh?"

His somber expression dropped momentarily, and he flashed his teeth at her in something akin to a smile.

She smiled back, and it was nearly genuine. Carson didn't mean any ill will. He was scared. Pretend as they might, the contrary was true; all the Hunters were frightened. They'd be out of their minds not to feel the fear. Carson thought Gemma could help and felt his duty was to ask for that help. She'd have probably done the same in his shoes. Boots.

"Truth is, I'd feel better out there if I had a partner," he admitted. "Something major's going on. Something..." his voice trailed off, and he shook his head.

Tapping her fingertips on the tabletop, she repeated firmly, "I'm out of that life, Carson." She took a deep breath and let it out slowly. "But if you're looking for someone to team up with, Randy Silverman is nearby."

Randy was an old family friend, and she was always happy to send a job his way, especially if there was a possibility it was paid work. That was a rarity, but it did happen every once in a while.

Carson let out a low whistle. He tilted his head and studied Gemma's face. "I've heard he's good."

Of course, Carson had heard Randy was good. Everyone in this town who was aware of the underworld roiling beneath their feet knew about Randy. Just like they knew about her parents.

Gemma nodded. "He's better than good. If it wasn't for Randy, my sister and I would probably both be dead right now," she confided.

She reached into her pocket and pulled out a pen. She

scribbled Randy's name and number on a nearby napkin and slid it to Carson.

He glanced down at it and then up at her. "Can I have his address? I prefer doing business in person."

"Obviously," Gemma remarked but added Randy's address to the napkin. "Make sure you tell him I sent you."

With a nod of thanks, Carson finally released her from the conversation. Gemma turned her attention back to her other customers. Even still, she couldn't shake the sinking feeling in her gut. She couldn't deny the signs. Writing the underworld off as something beneath their feet was extremely sugarcoating. The forces of evil had begun seeping into their world eons earlier, and now, their world teemed with it. It lurked around every corner, creeping amongst them, and one day she wouldn't be able to ignore it anymore.

But not today, she thought.

She shuddered as an imagined breath caressed the back of her neck.

"You look like you're deep in thought," a voice said from behind her.

She recognized the voice instantly.

It was Matt.

But still, her heart pounded, panicked, in her chest, as she whirled around to face him. He was standing less than a foot away from her. She'd really lost her touch if someone could sneak up on her that easily, which was proof enough for her that she would be more of a hindrance than a help to the Hunters. With that in mind, she more easily shoved the conversation she'd had with Carson aside. Resolving to pay more attention to her surroundings from now on, she turned her complete focus onto Matt with an easy, soft smile that didn't betray a hint of the darkness in her mind.

"You have another good turnout tonight," Matt remarked. Then he whispered, "Can I kiss you here, or would that be unprofessional?"

"No one's paying attention to us." She grabbed him gently by the front of his shirt and pulled him close. He lowered his head and brushed his lips against hers. When they broke apart, he grinned down at her. Her rapid pulse melted into a thrumming purr that spread throughout her body.

"How was your day, babe?" she asked. She took his hand and led him over to the open end of the bar for a moment of privacy away from the crowd.

Matt had recently branched out on his own after working unfulfilled as a junior journalist at the local paper for too long. He'd founded an online news outlet, which was going exceptionally well thus far. There was no better part of Gemma's day than listening to Matt passionately discuss his new venture. She was proud of him, and his happiness made her happy.

He lit up, his voice animated. "I think I found the story to make us a household name, Gems. It's going to be my big break. It took some digging, but I discovered a suspected serial killer is on the loose."

His eyes shone with excitement she usually found contagious. Still, a suspected serial killer wasn't something to get excited about.

Morbid curiosity piqued, she leaned in close, not wanting the other Hunters in the bar to overhear. "Tell me everything."

"Well, I know that all the victims have been men. And the cops are struggling to find any leads, much less solve the case."

"So there's not much for you to investigate, then?" Gemma asked, trying to keep her voice neutral, to keep him from hearing the relief she felt. She wanted to be supportive, but she'd be lying to them both if she acted like she wouldn't prefer if Matt stuck to stories that didn't involve men being murdered.

Matt's smile bordered on smug as he shook his head, clearly pleased with himself. "Oh, there's plenty for me to investigate." He dropped his voice to a conspiratorial whisper. "The bodies all have the same marking painted on their skin. I've heard murmurings that the murders may be a part of some kind of satanic ritual. Some kind of sacrifice. Have you ever heard of anything like that happening around here before?"

Gemma swallowed hard.

Matt knew about her past. There wasn't anything to hide, but still, Gemma felt uneasy. She'd heard of many things she didn't necessarily want to ever share with Matt. She tried to shield him from the darkness in this world.

"Markings?" she asked. "That's a little vague. It could be anything. Do you have a more accurate description?"

She hoped he didn't, but those hopes were dashed when he said, "Even better."

Matt pulled out his phone from his pocket and showed her a picture. Gemma glanced at it. Around her, the bar dimmed, everything in her periphery vision growing blurry and distant.

"I paid the coroner five hundred for this picture of his drawing. I hoped to research the markings and find something online, but…"

Matt's voice trailed off, and Gemma wanted nothing more than to be a regular girlfriend. Her automatic reaction was to scold Matt for spending five hundred dollars as if it was nothing. Neither of them was poor, but they weren't rich either. Especially since they were both self-employed, they couldn't afford to throw money around irresponsibly.

But at that moment, Gemma couldn't care less about what they could or couldn't afford.

Her breath caught in her throat. She rubbed at her neck as if pushing off imaginary ropes being wrapped around her throat to strangle her. A cold chill ran through her.

That's a witch's signature.

It comprised symbols indicative of rare ancient magic darker than any Hollywood filmmaker could imagine and splay on the screens of theaters across the country.

Not only was Matt way out of his depth, but so were the cops.

She put a hand over the phone and pushed it down out of view of anyone else. "I think you should find a different story," she said her voice firm. "An open police investigation into a suspected serial killer is not something I feel comfortable with you getting wrapped up in."

"Gemma, I run The Daily Truth, not The Daily Good News," Matt said.

"Matt, I mean it."

But instead of discouraging Matt, the look on her face and the tone in her voice only did the opposite. Smiling eagerly, he leaned even closer. "You know what this is." He removed the phone from her fingers and tapped the screen. "Don't you?"

She tugged at an errant curl in a nervous gesture while studiously avoiding his eyes. "Maybe," she hedged. She didn't want to start lying to Matt again, not when she'd only recently come clean with him about who she was. But she would do whatever it took to keep him safe. "The marking is familiar, but I can't be sure where I've seen it before," she said vaguely, trying to figure out how to keep him from digging further into this.

Matt put one hand on her face and forced her to look at him. "Gems, people need to know what's going on. That's why I set out on my own path, remember? I'm sick of the news being bought and paid for. The public has a right to know what they do not report at all, and even when it is, it's never a hundred percent accurate."

She shook her head, her heart beating rapidly. "This is something the public doesn't need to know." She couldn't keep the urgency she felt from flooding her voice as she spoke. "Not now and not with you at the helm. Please leave this one alone, Matt."

Dropping his hands, he sucked his bottom lip between his teeth for a moment before letting it fall back into place. "So, basically, you're asking me to bury a story," he said. "A story you know more about than you're letting on."

She shook her head again. "I'm not asking you to bury anything. I'm just asking you not to pursue it. I'm *begging* you not to pursue it."

She fell silent but held his gaze, her eyes pleading with him in a way her words couldn't.

He let out a sigh. "That would make me just like everybody else, Gems. Another good-for-nothing cog in the dishonest wheel. I'm not going to back down from this. Not this time. I'm sorry."

"But—"

"Listen. Do you support me or not?" he asked imploringly.

That's not fair, she thought. He knew she supported him. She'd been the one who'd encouraged him to go out on his own.

Frustrated, Gemma closed her eyes and counted to ten.

How could she make Matt understand the potential danger he was in?

If she told him they weren't dealing with a run-of-the-mill homicidal maniac who maybe dabbled in the occult, it would only intrigue him more. He obviously wasn't ready to listen to reason. She couldn't risk accidentally letting anything slip out that might spur him on.

She and Matt rarely disagreed, but when they did, she'd quickly learned it was best to take a step back and let each other cool off. She knew love wasn't all roses and rainbows. Still, she'd been through enough fights to last a lifetime. She wanted to keep her relationship with Matt as conflict-free as possible.

Taking a breath, she rose from where she'd been seated next to him and rounded the bar.

"Where are you going?" Matt asked from his stool on the other side. "I need you to tell me what you know."

"No. You need to take a beat before this gets heated. And so do I. Go home. I'll clean up here and talk to you later."

And please don't do anything stupid in the meantime.

She demanded he let the matter rest until they could really discuss it. Still, she knew doing so would likely only goad him into diving in headfirst before she even had a chance to think up a convincing argument against it.

"Okay," he said, the word thick with reluctance. "But… we're okay?"

God, the way he looked at her. She could tell he not only saw her but liked what he saw. No, he more than liked it. It was even more than love. It was acceptance, whole and pure.

"We're okay," she said, gently caressing his cheek.

We're okay, and I just have to find a way to keep us okay. To keep you okay.

He gathered his things and kissed her goodbye.

Gemma watched Matt leave and then turned to find Drew eyeing her.

"What?" she asked the bartender.

Drew shook her head. "I didn't say anything."

"Oh, your eyes were talking, lady." Gemma wagged her finger at Drew.

"You two are okay, right?" Drew asked a fretful note in her tone that matched the concern in her eyes.

"Eavesdrop much?" Gemma retorted, keeping her tone light. She mentally rolled back through the conversation with Matt. She wondered if they'd said anything that might get the supernatural gossip mill going.

"Gemma, by trade, I'm supposed to hear everything. It's part of the job description." Drew shrugged.

Had she heard the part about satanic rituals, though?

Gemma couldn't stomach the thought of Matt investigating those murders further. Still, it was a hornet's nest no one in town needed to kick, not even the most skilled Hunters, until they knew more. Drew was named after Nancy Drew, but Gemma didn't know whether she shared her namesake's penchant for amateur sleuthing. She hoped not.

"By the way," Gemma shifted the subject. "I never got my coke."

"By the way," Drew shot back. "You're a lousy tipper."

"Oh, I've got a tip for you," Gemma teased. "Your trash is overflowing."

Gemma pulled the garbage bag from the can under the bar and shook it at Drew,

who rolled her eyes. "I was getting to it."

"No worries," Gemma grinned. "I've got it."

It wasn't rare that Gemma jumped in and did the dirty work. All her employees knew she'd never ask them to do anything she wasn't willing to do herself. She had brought this bar to life with her own sweat, tears, and elbow grease, but it took a whole team to run it, and she was a team player. She was not too high and mighty to wash dishes or scrub the bathrooms.

"Thanks. Your coke will be waiting when you return," Drew promised.

"Give it a lime twist, please," Gemma requested before she headed through the kitchen to the back door.

As the cool early evening air hit her, she reviewed her conversation with Matt again. Gemma shuddered, recalling the coroner's drawing of the symbols painted on the corpse's skin.

Corpses, she corrected herself.

Matt hadn't said how many victims there had been, but he'd said serial killer, which meant at least three.

She would have to make him see reason.

Being close to the investigation meant being close to the killer—to the witch—and she couldn't let anything happen to him.

She pushed the thought away.

She couldn't lose anyone else.

She *wouldn't* lose anyone else.

Gemma closed in on the dumpster, and her nostrils twitched as she caught a whiff of a vile odor. She recoiled and dropped the trash bags to the ground, instinctively covering her mouth and nose with her hand. Her stomach lurched with her last meal threatening to come back up.

She knew from traumatic memory what she smelled wasn't garbage.

Swallowing hard, she took a step back and scanned the area.

Her brain screamed at her to turn and run, but her

body froze, unable to move. The hairs on her neck stood on end.

She blinked, trying to make sense of what she was seeing.

A mud-caked pair of construction-grade boots were sticking out from behind the dumpster.

Gemma knew those boots. And the dead man still wearing them.

***

Don't miss the next chapter in Gemma's epic battle against darkness. Get Book 2 now and hold your breath!

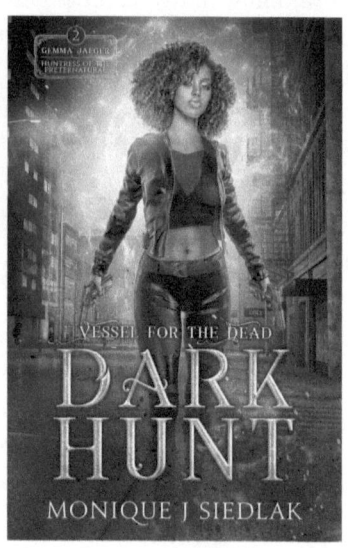

mojosiedlak.com/dark-hunt

JOIN MY
NEWSLETTER
GET UPDATES,
FREEBIES &
GIVEAWAYS
MOJOSIEDLAK.COM/NOCTURNECHRONICLES

SUPPORT ME BY LEAVING A REVIEW!

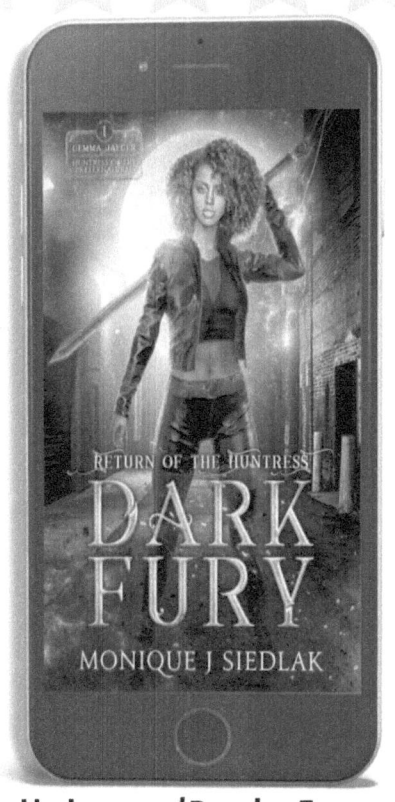

mojosiedlak.com/Dark_Fury_Book

JOIN MY
NEWSLETTER
GET UPDATES,
FREEBIES &
GIVEAWAYS
MOJOSIEDLAK.COM/NOCTURNECHRONICLES

About the Author

Monique J. Siedlak, a versatile author, seamlessly weaves mysticism and spirituality into her storytelling. With a background in Wicca, African Spirituality and Self Help, she's authored over 80 books under her full name.

In urban fantasy, her **Gemma Jaeger: Huntress of the Preternatural** series blurs reality and the uncanny, introducing a world where supernatural beings coexist with daily life. Vampires, werewolves, and witches walk city streets, brought to life by Monique's unique narrative style.

If you love shows like Supernatural, Grimm and Buffy the Vampire Slayer, her work is a perfect fit, merging supernatural allure with gritty urban realities.

Join her devoted readers and step into the preternatural with Monique.

facebook.com/moniquejsiedlak

instagram.com/monique_j_siedlak_author

twitter.com/moniquejsiedlak

tiktok.com/@moniquejsiedlak